Walter Bishop Mant

Christopheros

And Other Poems

Walter Bishop Mant

Christopheros
And Other Poems

ISBN/EAN: 9783337195267

Printed in Europe, USA, Canada, Australia, Japan

Cover: Foto ©Andreas Hilbeck / pixelio.de

More available books at **www.hansebooks.com**

CHRISTOPHEROS

AND OTHER POEMS

BY WALTER B. MANT

ARCHDEACON OF DOWN

LONDON

BELL AND DALDY 186 FLEET STREET

1861

T

THE Poems in this volume have been written (with some others) at various periods of life, from 1825 to 1861, and sometimes at considerable intervals of time. They have been composed, chiefly in the open air, as subjects or thoughts occurred, without any intention of publication; and are now printed at the suggestion of friends.

Hillsborough, Ireland.
August, 1861.

CONTENTS.

CONTENTS.

CHRISTOPHEROS.

SAINT CHRISTOPHER is represented as a man of gigantic stature, leaning on a staff, and carrying a little child, whose head is circled with a glory, through a swollen torrent. The legend, which seems to embody a fine allegory, and of which the following is a version, is to be found in Mrs. Jameson's "Sacred and Legendary Art."

PART I.

THE Kaiser feasted in his hall
    The Bosphorus beside;
    Around him knights and nobles sate
In rich Byzantine pride.
In stalk'd the Giant Opheros,
    And bended not his knee:—
" I seek the mightiest Prince on earth,
    " They tell me thou art he!"

B

The Kaiser smiled,—" Wherever Rome
  " Hath sent her eagles forth,
" From Afric's burning deserts to
  " The forests of the North,—
" From Persia's eastern boundary
  " To Britain's western land,—
" We know no tribe that braves our power,
  " Or questions our command."

" Long have I sought," the Giant spoke,
  " A master to obey ;
" But ne'er would bend except to one
  " Who bears the mightiest sway.
" While thou doft reign on earth supreme,
  " And for no foe dost quail,
" Thy bidding, Kaiser, will I do,
  " Nor in my service fail."

Long time that giant servèd there
  With deeds of wond'rous might ;
He did the Kaiser's hest by day,
  He watch'd his gate at night :—
He scorn'd the pomp and show of courts,
  He reck'd not of the cheer,—
His food the simplest fruits of earth,
  His drink the fountain clear.

The Kaiser sate within his hall ;—
  With verse and legend wild
Of combats with the Evil One
  A bard the hours beguiled :
And ever, as the HATEFUL NAME
  Was utter'd in the lay,
The Kaiser cross'd himself, and cried,
  " GOD shield us from his sway !"

Outspake the Giant Opheros—
  " And who is this," he said,
" At whom the mightiest Prince on earth
  " Doth seem so sore dismay'd ?"
" The Prince of evil spirits, who
  " From heaven once was hurl'd,—
" And now the Prince of Darkness—the
  " Usurper of the world."

Outspake the Giant Opheros,
  " I here renounce my vow,—
" I will serve the Prince of Darkness, he
  " Is mightier than thou !"
He deign'd no further leave-taking,
  He turn'd himself from all ;—
And the Prince of Darkness met him
  As he strode from out the hall.

Part II.

He travell'd with a mighty train ;
　　All kinds of men were there,—
The nobles, and the peasant folk—
　　Strong men, and women fair :
The Giant met him boldly, and
　　He bended not his knee,—
" I seek the mightiest Prince on earth,—
　　I hear that thou art he !"

Loud laugh'd the Fiend—" Where shines the sun,
　　" Where'er the waters roll,
" I claim the born allegiance
　　" Of every human soul :—
" Mine are the kingdoms of the earth—
　　" To me they homage pay,—
" And neither King nor Kaiser
　　" Can free them from my sway !"

" Long have I sought," quoth Opheros,
　　" A master to obey,
" But scorn to bend except to him
　　" Who bears the widest sway.

" While thou art mightiest on earth,
   " And for no foe dost quail,
" I will serve thee, Prince of Darkness,
   " Nor in my service fail !"

The Giant served the Evil One
   For many a weary day ;
Full soon he loathed the servitude,
   But still he must obey.
He was sick of fleshly pleasure—
   Was sick of deeds of blood,—
Sick of the fiendish laugh and sneer
   That scorn'd at all things good.

One morn they met a Pilgrim grey,
   Who loudly thus did sing,—
" Rejoice, for CHRIST is risen, and
   " Of glory He is King !"
The Foul One trembled sorely,
   His proud eye 'gan to quail,
The sneer hath left his fallen lip,
   His dusky cheek is pale !

Outspake the Giant Opheros,—
   " And who is this," he said,
" At whose name the Prince of Darkness
   Shows signs of mortal dread ?"

The Foul one falter'd—" One who cares
  " For neither mine nor me ;—
" He calls himself the King of kings,
  " My mortal enemy !"

Outspake the Giant Opheros—
  " I here renounce my vow,
" I will serve this King of kings, for He
  " Is mightier than thou !"
He spat before him on the ground,
  The cross in air he traced ;
And the Christian Pilgrim follow'd he
  As slowly on he paced.

PART III.

" GOD speed thee !" quoth the Giant then.
  " Christ save thee, Sir !" he cried ;
And courteously, and brotherly,
  They travell'd side by side.
" And tell me now," quoth Opheros,
  " Where dwells the mighty King,
" Whose name makes Satan tremble, and
  " Whose glory thou dost sing ?"

" It is CHRIST, the King of glory,
   " His dwelling is in Heaven :
" To Him all power in heaven and earth
   " By GOD most high is given."
" Him would I seek," said Opheros,
   " And give Him service free ;
" I seek to serve the mightiest king—
   " I feel that this is He !"

" Him must thou serve," the Pilgrim said,
   " With fasting and with prayer :
" Him must thou serve with loving heart,
   " And do His will with care."
" I cannot fast, it suits me not,
   " I never learnt to pray ;
" But I will serve with cheerful heart,
   " With labour night and day."

The Christian Pilgrim wonder'd sore
   That stalwart form to see,
Who never yet to GOD in prayer
   Had learn'd to bow the knee :—
But he thought him of a proverb old,—
   " To labour is to pray ;"
And he said, " If thou wilt serve the King,
   " I will thee show the way."

They travell'd on in friendly talk
    Until, across the road,
Down from a deep and rocky glen,
    A mountain-torrent flow'd ;
There was no bridge across the stream,
    The bank was high and steep,—
And the Giant bore the Pilgrim o'er
    The current wide and deep.

" Be this thy task," the Pilgrim said,—
    " In yonder rocky cell,
" In silence and in loneliness,
    " A season must thou dwell ;
" And bear across this torrent wide
    " Each traveller on his way,
" Until the King shall call thee, whom
    " Thou wishest to obey."

In silence and in loneliness
    The Giant sojourn'd there,
And many a way-worn traveller
    Across the stream did bear :
Full cheerfully he bore them o'er,
    Then shared his simple food,
And, as he served his fellow-men,
    He deem'd the service good.

He mark'd the sun that shone aloft,
  With blessing for the light;
He mused with awe upon the stars
  That lit the skies by night:—
He watch'd the beasts that roam'd the woods,
  The birds that wing'd the air;
And long'd to know the mighty Power
  That made all things so fair!

He ponder'd on his wasted hours
  Within the Kaiser's hall,
He shudder'd at his deeds of sin,
  The Prince of Darkness' thrall;
For light and pardon in his soul
  An anxious longing felt,—
And bow'd the heart that ne'er had pray'd,
  The knee that ne'er had knelt!

PART IV.

THERE came at length a stormy night,
  And wildly blew the blast;
The moon with clouds was hidden,
  The rain was falling fast;

But still a light forth twinkled from
   The Giant-hermit's cell,
And, broken by the eddies, on
   The rushing torrent fell.

Out look'd the Giant Opheros
   Upon the stormy sky;
And hark! his ear was startled
   By a weak and distant cry.
He listen'd, and he thought he heard
   A voice that call'd his name;
Though faint and feeble, yet he deem'd
   Across the stream it came.

Uptook the Giant Opheros
   His staff of holly tree,
And across the foaming torrent
   He hath waded to the knee.
The moon shone out amid the clouds,
   And, by the waters wild,
He saw, upon the rocky bank,
   Where sat *a little Child.*

" Wilt thou bear me o'er the waters
   " For the love of CHRIST?" he cried.
" That will I," answer'd Opheros,
   " Whatever may betide!"

The Child he took upon his arm,—
  Small child and light was he;—
And through the foaming waters
  He waded to the knee.

But scarcely had he carried him
  Three fathoms from the shore,
That Child became a heavier load
  Than aught he ever bore :
A strange and wondrous burden
  His mighty strength oppress'd,
And in mid stream the waters rose
  Until they reach'd his breast.

" What art thou, little Child ?" he cried ;
  " My burden weighs me down :
" And the water-floods are rising fast ;
  " I fear they will us drown !"
" Fear not the torrent," said the CHILD,
  " It flows at My command ;
" And I measure ocean's waters
  " In the hollow of My hand !

" I bore the sins of humankind,—
  " Thou canst not bear thine own ;—
" The Arm that governs earth and heav'n
  " Is round thy shoulder thrown :—

———

" Thou walkest through the waters safe,
   " For I with thee will go ;
" And, though thou passest through the floods,
   " They shall not overflow !"

That little CHILD upraised His hand,
   And bade the storm to cease ;
Then fell the blast, the night was past,
   And all was light and peace ;
Scarce ankle-deep the water flow'd,
   Until they reach'd the land,
And the Giant set his burden down
   Above the river strand.

Forthwith he struck into the earth
   His staff of holly tree,
And down before that little Child
   He fell on bended knee.
" Long have I waited Thee," he cried ;
   " Thou calledst me by my name ;
" I worship Thee, the King of kings,—
   " What service dost Thou claim ?"

" Yes ! thou hast served Me patiently,
   " In silence and alone,—
" Hast learnt from Nature's works My power
   " And providence to own ;

" Hast felt the burden of thy sins,
    " And, in afliction's tide,
" Hast learnt to bear the cross of Christ,
    " And My protection tried.

" Arise, and take thy staff!" He rose
    From humbly bended knee,
And turn'd where in the earth he struck
    The staff of holly tree ;
Another wonder greets his eyes,—
    The holly staff was green,
And leaves had grown, and flow'rs had blown,
    And berries ripe were seen.

Once more He spoke : " When in the heart
    " I see the seeds of grace,
" I love to watch and nourish it,
    " And make it grow apace ;
" And I revive the deaden'd heart,
    " Again I make it shoot
" With signs of life, and flowers of faith,
    " And love's perfected fruit.

" And I accept thy service now
    " To bear a higher part ;
" As thou hast borne Me in thine arms
    " So bear Me in thine heart ;

―――――

" Learn now unto thy fellow-men
   " My mercies to proclaim ;
" Be CHRIST the burden of thy speech,—
   " CHRISTOPHEROS thy name !"

THE HAPPY ISLAND.

A CLASSICAL LEGEND.

THE small Island of Leuce, in the Euxine, was one of the spots fixed on by poets for the habitation of heroes after death. Being considered sacred, it was rarely visited ; but there is a tradition that one favoured seaman, having fallen asleep on the shore, was wakened by Achilles, and conveyed to a splendid pavilion, where a banquet was prepared.

The Symplegades, (line 2,) also called Cyaneæ, or Blue Rocks, were two rocks at the entrance of the Euxine, which were supposed to float, and crush any ship that tried to sail between them. The optical illusion was broken by the passage of the Argonauts.

THE galley, with the sunset breeze,
  Hath pass'd the blue Symplegades,
    Those magic rocks, that float no more
Since Argo sought the Colchian shore,
Fraught with the hero-sons of Greece,
And bore away the wondrous fleece.
Behind old Hæmus' ridge of snows
The sun's last setting radiance glows ;

And, 'neath the glorious summer sky,
　Secure, and free from fear,
The bark glides on all tranquilly,
　As if no storm were near.

But rougher now the wave is growing,
Fresher now the breeze is blowing,
And swiftly o'er the dark blue sea
The clouds are gathering fearfully.
Thicker grows the storm around,
Loud the thunder-peals resound,
And, through the awful face of night,
The lightning flashes red and bright;
Two nights, two days their course they run,
　Thick mists around them lay;
By night no star, by day no sun
　To show their dangerous way.

But, ere the second day was o'er,
Sudden was hush'd the tempest's roar;
The wind had sunk, the storm was gone,
Bright through the clouds the sunbeams shone,
And all was tranquil, save the sea, .
Which swell'd and sunk tumultuously;
Yet, heaving still its troubled breast,
Was sinking, by degrees, to rest.
And where in peace the galley lay,
　An island rose to view,

On which his loveliest lingering ray
  The setting Day-god threw.

Now five have left the vessel's side
To seek where living waters glide ;
The Master, keener than the rest,
With bolder foot pursued his quest ;
He left the margin of the sea,
Whose waves were rippling peacefully,
He pass'd a mazy, pathless wood,
And there in silent transport stood ;
For scenes, not of the haunts of men,
  And strange to mortal eyes,
Entranced his fascinated ken
  With longing and surprise.

Before him lay an emerald mead,
With golden flow'rets overspread ;
Beyond, a lake of silvery sheen,
Its banks all clothed with myrtles green,
Where, glistening in the moon's full light,
A streamlet pour'd its waters bright.
He reach'd the lake ; its mossy shore
With sweetest flowers was spangled o'er,
With sweetest flowers the boughs were hung,
  While, to the streamlet near,
The night-birds' songs harmonious rung
  In music soft and clear.

c

No sight but beautiful was near,
No sound but melody was here,
And every breath, with sweetness fraught,
New rapture to his senses brought.
With awful joy he gazed around :
Save his, he wist, that holy ground
No mortal foot had ever prest,—
It was the Island of the Blest!
Too much that thought for mortal's soul ;—
    For very joy he wept :—
A soothing languor o'er him stole,
    And, as he gazed, he slept!

A touch awakes him! Who is near?
A form to reverence, not to fear ;
Of stature tall, of mighty frame,
A step of pride, an eye of flame,
Yet temper'd by a smile as sweet
As lover's tenderest wish should meet ;
Above his brows and forehead fair
In ringlets stream'd his auburn hair,
Press'd lightly by a golden ring ;—
    The blissful soil he trod,
In majesty of port a king,
    In form a demigod.

" Arise," he cried, " to thee, of Heaven
" Most rarely-favour'd man, 'tis given

" To view the seats to men unknown,
" Reserved for Virtue's sons alone.
" By few this Island is beheld ;
" To fewer are its joys unveil'd ;
" To few is given the will to dare,
" The heart resolved to do or bear ;—
" Such gifts have led thy steps aright
  " On this adventurous quest ;
" And in the Happy Isle to-night
  " Thou art Achilles' guest.''

He led him through groves of myrtle fair,
Whose sweetness fill'd the evening air,
  Till they enter'd together a garden's bound,
Where the loveliest flowers were growing round,
And the sweetest shrubs their odours lent,
And the tenderest birds their voices blent,
And the leaves were moved by the gentlest air,
And peacefully couch'd the deer and hare,
  And the wildest beasts were tame and still,
    For discord here must cease ;
  That holy Isle could bear no ill,
    But all was love and peace !

Hard by the margin of the wood
A lordly, bright pavilion stood,
Whose doors of cedar, hinged with gold,
In courteous guise their leaves unroll'd.

" Here enter!" thus the Hero said,
" And here thy wandering steps be stay'd!
" Immortal hands shall spread the feast
" In kinduess to a mortal guest ;
" Immortal forms shall grace the board,
   " And bid thee welcome here!
" And strains, from lips immortal pour'd,
   " Shall fill thy charmèd ear."

Within the softly-lighted hall,
Where the rays from perfumed cressets fall,
The Inmates of the Happy Isle
Welcome the stranger with a smile ;
And Thetis, ocean-born, is there,
And Agamemnon's daughter fair,
Iphigenia, whom of yore
From death the pitying Goddess bore ;
And Ajax' noble form is here,
   His sorrows at an end ;
And brave Patroclus' visage clear,
   Rejoicing in his friend.

Ambrosial dainties deck the board,
By hero-hands is nectar pour'd ;
And, when the feast is o'er, his lyre,
Saved from the spoil of Thebæ's fire,[1]
Achilles takes, and sings the praise
Of heroes in such thrilling lays,

That, as the strains ascend more high,
Mute sit that glorious company ;
Patroclus stands with eye intent;
  The Stranger, heart and ears
On that entrancing music bent,
  Finds sweet relief in tears!

The song is o'er,—to needful rest
The Hero leads his wearied guest;
With softest skins the couch is spread,
Soft sleep descends upon his head :—
O wake not! Why return again
To mortal toil and mortal pain?
But earth demands the mortal's share
Of human toil and human care;
And glimpses of Elysian light
  May cheer the darksome way,
But, lest they strain the dazzled sight,
  Must shine with chasten'd ray.

And so, the blissful vision o'er,
He waken'd by the lake's lone shore;
The stream, the mead, the flow'rets bright
Were glittering in the orient light;
He rose, bewilder'd and amazed,
Once more with transport round him gazed,
And, blessing the benignant Heaven
That had such hopes, such visions given,

He sought his comrades on the shore,
  His vessel on the wave,
The toils of life to bear once more,
  The ills of life to brave.

1827.

THE BATTLE OF SALAMIS.

A BALLAD OF GRECIAN HISTORY.[2]

ARISE ! ye sons of Greece, arise !
　　" And free your fatherland ;
　　" And save your children and your wives ;
　　" The foe is on your strand !

　　" Strike for the Temples of your Gods,
　　　" And free their altar-fires ;
　　" The tombs of heroes famed of yore,
　　　" The ashes of your sires !

　　" Ye *now* must strike for all ye love,
　　　" The foe is on your strand :
　　" Arise, ye sons of Greece, arise !
　　　" And save your fatherland !"

So rung the inspiring sounds that roused
　　The Grecians, few, but brave,
When Persia's thousand galleys lay
　　Proud threatening on the wave.

Those thousand galleys lay display'd
  Before their Monarch's throne,
And countless armies stood around;
  And *all* that Monarch's own !

The sun arose on Salamis,
  And fell across the bay
On banner, turban, bow and shield,
  The Persian's rich array;

Behind, on helm and spear it glanced,
  On mail-clad warriors shone;
And few, but firm, in close array,
  The Grecian fleet came on.

The Invaders deem'd that unprepared,
  Secure they held their prize;
They heard, appall'd, the patriot shout,—
  " Ye sons of Greece, arise !"

The sun, before he set that night,
  Look'd down upon the bay,
And Persian wrecks and Persian dead
  Beneath him scatter'd lay;

And Xerxes' golden throne was gone,
  His hosts had left the strand;
The free-born sons of Greece had risen,
  And saved their fatherland!

'DONOHUE comes to his secret Tower,
He opens the door with a word of power,
And he stands within the charmèd
    bound,
And his dark eye scans the chamber round.
'Tis here he holds his commune high,
With beings hid from unaided eye,
And calls the spirits of wood and rill,
And lake and mountain, to do his will.
He comes—but he comes not alone to-night,
For by his side was a Lady bright,
As fair, as slight as the jasmine flower
That waves at the window of her bower,—
Yet she looks around that chamber lone
With an eye as proud as the Chieftain's own.

Much of wonder, I ween, was there
Might daunt the heart of a lady fair;
With its darksome walls, and its iron door,
And the fretted roof, and the marble floor,
And the cresset that hung from the centre beam
Casting beneath but a fitful gleam ;—

Whence it borrow'd that ghastly ray,
" Well may I guess, though I dare not say;"—
Traced on the floor was a magic ring,
And she look'd thereon without shuddering,
Though the circle was form'd with the bones of the
        dead,
And each cardinal point was a grisly head !

The lake beneath the casement lay,
She saw the moonbeams on it play,—
She look'd aloft—the sky was bright,
No cloud obscured the face of night :
She look'd on the Chieftain's face, and smiled,—
But his brow was clouded, his eye was wild,
And she felt a thrill through her bosom spread,
And a deeper glow on her cheek was shed,
As his full deep voice the silence broke,
And thus in solemn accents spoke :—

" Thou hast sought to know my skill ;
" I have sworn to grant thy will ;
" Rashly thy request was made—
" Rashly was my promise said !
" Knowest thou what forms of dread
" Soon will flit around thy head ?
" Knowest thou what sounds of fear
" Soon will strike upon thine ear ?

" Sights of death, and sounds of hell—
" Such as tongue may never tell !
" Bravest men can scarcely brook
" On these dismal sights to look,—
" Warriors, in dire dismay,
" At these sounds have shrunk away ;
" Can thy woman's spirit bear,
" Such to see, and such to hear ?

" Yes !—I see thy kindling eye
" Tells thy purpose fix'd and high :
" Come then to the magic ring,
" While the mighty charms I sing ;
" But beware no sight nor sound
" Tempt thee from its circling bound.
" There no evil can assail thee,—
" But beware lest courage fail thee !
" Whatsoever meets thy sight—
    " Whatsoever strikes thine ear—
" Though thou faintest with affright—
    " Utter not a sound of fear ;
" Else falls the spirits' wrath on me,
" And sorrow must thy portion be !"

They enter'd the circle—he open'd the book—
That instant with thunder the chamber shook,
Though a moment before the sky was fair,
And there was not a cloud in the moonlit air.

He read from the volume the words of power :
To its base was shaken the darksome Tower ;
Smother'd by clouds was the full moon's beam,
But the lightning flash'd with a lurid gleam,
And the mystic circle was girt with flame,
Which, lightning-lit, from the pavement came !

But the Lady still look'd on,
    And her proud eye did not quail,
Though her brow was cold as stone,
    And her cheek was deadly pale.

And louder and nearer the thunder came,
And higher and redder arose the flame,
Then sunk with a sudden, crashing sound,
And all was stillness and darkness round.
Harder that stillness—that darkness—to bear
Than the thunder's crash, or the flame's red glare ;
For the Chieftain's voice, as his charms he read,
Scarce broke the depth of that silence dread ;
And scarcely the cresset's feeble ray
Reach'd to the book that beneath it lay !

Yet she stood as still as death,
    With proud, unshrinking eye,
Though quicker came her breath,
    And her heart beat loud and high.

The Chieftain with steady voice read on,
And fiery eyes through the darkness shone ;
And hideous faces appear'd to rise,
Seen by the light of their own red eyes ;
Birds of ill-omen, with clanging wing,
Flew with loud screams round the charmèd ring ;
Serpents and scorpions were creeping about ;
Sounds of torment and death rang out ;
Devilish laughter, and scornful hiss—
Darkness and silence were better than this !

    Yet still she dared to look,
        Nor turn'd aside her head,
    Though her eyelid quivering shook,
        And her lip was blanch'd with dread.

Trembling she clung to the Chieftain's arm ;
Still he went on with his mighty charm :
Up like a curtain the darkness drew,
And a vision more horrid was now in view.
The light of the cresset was high and red,
And a human form was beneath it spread ;
And it seem'd that demons, with murderous knife,
Were sportively spilling the stream of life !
Sudden they fled from the work of death—
Heavens ! 'twas her child that lay beneath !

    One piercing cry—no more—
        From her bursting bosom came,

As sunk on the marble floor
The Lady's fainting frame.

Still in that deathlike trance she lay
Till the sky was red with the breaking day,
And the sun arose, with his joyous beam,
And glanced on the lake and the silver stream,
And through the turret casement shone
On the forms that lay on the floor of stone.
Slowly the Lady shuddering woke,
Her frame with thrilling horror shook;
She gazed with haggard look and wild,
   And, pillow'd on her arm,
She saw her own, her only, child
In peaceful sleep, he sweetly smiled,
   Unscathed, and free from harm;
And the mother's tears of trembling joy
Fell on the cheek of the lovely boy.

But far, alas! from his father's home
O'Donohue's infant heir must roam;
For never again from that dread hour
Return'd the Lord of the darksome Tower;
And kinsmen, careless of the right,
Usurp'd his lands with impious might.
Never again on heath or green
O'Donohue's stately form was seen:
Never did he his steed bestride

To chase the stag on Killarney's side:
Never again did the trumpet's breath
Sound to his charge on the field of death:
Never again in peaceful hall
Did minstrels rise at the Chieftain's call,
To sing their proud unfetter'd lays
With the harp's wild note to their master's praise!

For now the spirits of lake and hill,
Whom he had bound to obey his will,
Have claim'd the forfeit of the spell,
And he is bound with them to dwell.
Yet still, at times, as peasants say,
When the dawn first breaks on the morn of May,
When the eddying winds, in their wild career,
The silvery foam from the waves uprear;
When the water-spirits delight to sweep
In dance uncouth o'er Killarney's deep—
Then is O'Donohue's spirit there,
His part in the shadowy troop to bear.
Proudly in front of the mystic train
His snow-white steed does the Chieftain rein,
And proudly gaze on the fairy sport,
As a king looks down on his royal court;
For they, whose captive he still must be,
Give honour due to his ancestry,
As when, the Lord of the darksome Tower,
He bound them to awe by his magic power!

IS sweet, when storms are raging on the
  " main,[5]
  " The sailors' labour from the shore to
    " see ;
" Not that thou joyest in another's pain,
  " But that 'tis pleasant in security
  " To view the ills from which thyself art free ;—
" 'Tis sweet again, when banner'd hosts engage,
  " To mark, the danger all unshared by thee,
" How men with men the deadly contest wage,
" To note the victors' pride, the vanquish'd's bootless
    " rage !

" But sweeter nought, than from the calm retreat
  " Raised by the sage's philosophic mind,
" To see the crowds of men beneath our feet,
  " To mark them wandering tost in mazes blind,
  " Striving the paths of life in vain to find !"
So thought the bard, whose soul's undaunted tone
  Dared spurn the creeds received by all his kind,
Dared half unseat the Almighty from His throne,
And raise from atoms wild a chance-world of his own.

I envy not that sceptic's station high,
　His " shrine serene " of philosophic pride,
From which he view'd with self-complacent eye
　His brethren's errors, only to deride;
　I envy not the skill by which he tried
To crush the hopes on which mankind reposed,
　And Heaven's preserving providence denied :—
Sweeter to me from Nature's book unclosed
To read His praise by whom the world is all disposed.

To stand among the everlasting hills,
　To listen to the breeze's sweeping tone,
To hear the music of the mountain rills,
　The lark's wild song, the plover's plaintive
　　moan,
　To wander on the ocean shore alone,
And watch the waves roll onward to the strand,
　While backward far the feathery spray is thrown ;
And thus, in all His works to view the Hand
That gave the sea his bounds, that bade the moun-
　　tain stand :—

These are delights which nought beside can give,
　These are the joys from boyhood dear to me ;
Then with intenser life I seem to live,
　My footstep feels more light, my breath more free :
　I cannot gaze upon the boundless sea,
Or what the mountain's towering height looks o'er,

But then a feeling of eternity
Swells in me from my bosom's inmost core,
And bids from earthly thoughts heavenward my
    spirit soar.

For who can view the extent of sea and sky
    While realms more distant still escape his glance,
Then turn upon himself his scrutiny,
    Nor tremble at his insignificance,
    A worm—an atom—in that vast expanse?
Yet should the thought move not thine awe alone,
    It rather should thy gratitude enhance,
To Him who from His all-o'er-ruling throne
Such proof of boundless love to thee, poor worm,
    hath shown!

On, then! where Nature in her wildest forms
    Presents a barrier to the Atlantic wave,
Which now, infuriate with the Northern storms,
    That barrier's rocky strength appears to brave;
    Now, calmly rippling, loves its base to lave;
Or rolls upon the strand in breakers wide;
    Or booms within the deep re-echoing cave:
Here let us roam awhile as chance may guide,
Nor sigh for fashion's haunts of pomp, and wealth,
    and pride.

Thou, CAUSEWAY OF THE GIANTS, be my theme;—
    Whether, as legendary tales maintain,

And scarcely false, I ween, the rustics deem,
   Great FIONN M'COUL and his gigantic train
   Bridged thus their way across the northern main,
From INNISFAIL to MORVEN's windy shore;[o]
   And, when to ERIN they return'd again,
Last of his host the Chieftain pass'd it o'er,
Then stampt it to the abyss, that none might cross
     it more.

Yet, in despite of modern architect,
   Unharm'd he left what we in wonder see,
Daring us pigmy mortals to erect
   A mole of equal strength and symmetry
   To this his masterpiece of masonry :—
Pause—pause—presumptuous strain !—no mortal
     hand
   Hath based those massive pillars in the sea,
Or caused yon colonnade on high to stand
Where foot of lightest bird may scarce find space to
     land.

Walk o'er the Causeway !—While thy footsteps tread
   Its wondrous pavement, downward cast thine eyes,
And as thou view'st it thus beneath thee spread,
   Mark how in all varieties of size,
   Angle, and form, that fancy could devise,
Without cement it hath compacted been
   So closely knit, that it almost defies

The edge of keenest steel to intervene,
Even " dark brown Luno's blade," the adjacent
    stones between.[7]

Or, taking here thy station by " the Loom,"[8]
  (Whose mighty frame surpassing that whereon
The " Fatal Sisters " wrought their web of doom,
    Seems fit for Giants' handicraft alone,
    For every thread is of columnar stone ;)
Mark how the Power that raised the colonnade
    In even joints divided hath each one,
And here concave above convex hath laid,
And here for rounded base an hollow'd cup hath
    made.

Yet vainly chisel held by mortal hand
    To carve that hard unyielding stone hath tried ;[9]
Nor e'er would mortal builder dare to stand
    Where, on that craggy promontory's side,
    Which hangs abruptly frowning o'er the tide
In blue magnificence beneath it spread,
    Thou see'st yon pillar'd range extending wide,
Which firmly based upon its ochre bed
Contrasts the dark basalt with tinge of liveliest red.

What then ? Did Nature in some secret throes,
    Some sudden burst of a volcanic shower,

This mighty fabric to the air expose,
　An age's wonder, in one little hour?
　Or aid its growth by crystallizing power?[10]
What need we thus inquire?　Enough to know
　That He who frames the texture of a flower,
And bids the oak from smallest acorn grow,
By His creative will hath rear'd the Causeway so.

Rest we awhile upon the GIANT's CHAIR,[11]
　Whence Fionn M'Coul, 'tis said, was wont to
　　view
His workmen's toil; and thence up PORT NA FHAIR
　Let us the steep and winding path pursue :—
　Or if thy foot be firm, thine eye be true,
With me thou may'st the narrow track assay,[12]
　Which, scarce distinguish'd from the cliff's dark
　　hue,
Sweeps round the bosom of each winding bay,
And round each headland's face points out a dizzy
　　way.

Yet, sooth to say, no path is this for him
　Who turns from danger or from toil aside,
Whose brain grows giddy, and whose senses swim,
　To see beneath him swell the boiling tide,
　As on yon ledge, now scarce a hand-breadth
　　wide,

We plant our footsteps, now with steady hand
   Grasping the rock we stretch the lengthen'd stride,
Now climb, and now descend, while full command
Of breast, and limb, and eye, the varied toils demand.

But who such dangerous pathway fear,
   (No carpet-knight the venturous feat may dare,)
Or who would shun the toil, may choose instead
   The steep but safe ascent of Port na Fhair,
   The " Shepherd's Pathway ;" child, or lady fair
May, fearless, climb it, and pursue the way
   Along the Headlands; thence what prospects fair
Greet the beholder! Shore, and winding bay,
And cliff's fantastic form, and columns' long array !

Pause we on RUE BEN VALLA : mighty wall
   By Nature rear'd, it hangs above the tide
Narrow and steep : a range of pillars tall
   Its eastward summit crown, its westward side
   The unform'd basaltic dyke : the bays beside
Contrasted strangely each with each appear ;
   Here PORT NA FHAIR, green, sloping, spacious,
      wide,
There PORT REOSTAN's wondrous Theatre
Contracted, narrow, steep, columnar, wild, and drear.

Our track lies round Reostan : on its verge,
   Eastward, the CHIMNEY'D HEADLAND for a space

Claims a delay.—Mark, how above the surge
  The storm-swept column rears aloft its face
  In lonely strength : observe its dizzy place,
Then think what courage *his*, what reckless mind,
  Who up yon cliff clomb to that column's base,
And left, in vaunting championship, behind
His gage of challenge there, ne'er touch'd but by the
      wind ![13]

Below, see PORT NA SPANIA ! Sad the hour[14]
  To Spain's proud king that gave the bay its name,
What time, with all his kingdom's warlike flower,
  Towards England's coasts the fierce ARMADA came,
  Threatening her peaceful homes with sword and
      flame ;
Trusting 'neath Rome's dark tyranny again
  The Island-heretics' free souls to tame,
And boasting England's navy sail'd in vain
To oppose the Pope-blest fleet sent forth by bigot
      Spain !

And vain perchance it had been ; but a Hand
  Mightier than Spain's had deign'd to interpose ;—
For, ere that fleet could near the fated land,
  The Word went forth, and straight the tempest
      rose,
  And far and wide dispersed the insulting foes ;

And England's navy, so despised before,
   Made havoc of the INVINCIBLES ;—of those
Who sail'd so gaily from LISBOA's shore
How few their shatter'd barks inglorious homeward
    bore !

The sun had set beneath the summer sea,
   The shades of evening now were gathering fast,
When, o'er the dark waves sailing gallantly,
   Hispania's enfign floating from her maft,
   Round dark BENGORE an armèd galley past,
All danger yet escaped :—and hark ! what sound
   Breaks the deep stillness ? The loud cannon's blast
Reverberates the hollow cliffs around,
And from the unconscious rocks the harmless balls
    rebound.

No ! not all harmless ! Heard ye not the crash
   The column, rent from its foundation, gave ?
And heard ye not the oft-repeated splash,
   As joint by joint it leapt into the wave ?
   But why this havoc ? Wherefore did the brave
Waste on the rocks their dread artillery's might ?
   Not with such senseless fury did they rave,
But thought, deceived by the declining light,
The towers of proud DUNLUCE were risen upon their
    sight.

Nor strange their error, for the seaman viewing
  How wild a seat Dunseverick's ruins hold,[15]
And westward thence at eve his course pursuing,
  Might deem the pillars on this headland bold
  To be the turrets of some fortress old ;
And thus the Spaniards deem'd, our legends say :
  But now the mists of night around them roll'd,
And on the waters all secure they lay ;—
But where was that good ship at dawn, and where
     were they ?

The evening-star beheld the vessel lie
  Silent as sleep—anon a crashing shock,
Then one unanimous heart-thrilling cry
  On the deep stillness of the midnight broke :
  Again she dash'd upon the hidden rock,
There groaning split,—and on the watery bed
  A shatter'd hull she lay : when morning woke
The bay with fragments of the wreck was spread,
The shore with broken spars, and corpses of the
     dead !

This was a Nation's loss ;—and thus they perish'd
  Far distant from their homes, their fate unknown
By those who might their dead remains have che-
     rish'd :—
  Sister, or wife, or mother, was there none,
  Might say of Port na Spania, with a groan,

"There died our friends!"—and yet, though strange
    it be,
These cliffs were witness to the death of one,
A peasant, which hath sadder seem'd to me
Than that disastrous wreck of Spain's proud chi-
    valry.

Alas, poor ADAM MORNING! doom'd to feel[16]
    How keen the gnawing tooth of penury;
He, bearing in his hand the scanty meal
    For the loved partner of his industry,
    Was here descending—still the spot ye see
Where, like the Organ of some Minster vast,
    Yon columns, knit with neatest symmetry,
Stand bedded in the cliff—so far he pass'd—
And there his footstep slipp'd—that footstep was his
    last!

Headlong he fell—and she beheld his fall,
    As on the shore she piled the seaweed's heap,
Their humble toil;—yet wist she not at all
    What thing it was that fell,—"a mountain-sheep
    Perchance had miss'd its footing on the steep:"—
But when at length she nearer drew, and there
    Beheld his mangled corpse, how did she weep,
How did she beat her breast, and rend her hair,
With all the frenzy wild of comfortless despair!

Such, as the fatal cliff each stranger spies,
　　The tale our rustical conductors tell :
Yet still a dangerous trade his grandson plies,
　　Nor shuns the cliff from which the grandsire fell.
　　So the Swiss hunter from his native dell,
Chasing the nimble-footed chamois goes,
　　Where 'midst the glacier's slippery heights they
　　　　dwell ;
Nor shuns the desperate leap, though well he knows
The death-place of his sires are those eternal snows !

On MADH-A-RUAGH's cliffs, in SPANIA's bay,
　　'Twere long to tell what wonders we behold,
Sublimely savage ! as we wend our way
　　Towards BEN ANOURAN's head ; nor needs be told
　　How from the summit of that headland bold
The steeps of PLAISKIN first we look upon :
　　Nor how, the jointless columns past, we hold
The track across the heather to BENBAWN,
The seat that bears thy name, ill-fated HAMILTON ![17]

Here, till we reach'd the well-selected place,
　　With eyes averted from the edge pursue [18]
The path :—we turn—and now the eastward face
　　Of PLAISKIN bursts at once upon our view !—
　　Ah me ! what words so fine, what pen so true,
As may the grandeur of that scene pourtray,
　　With every varying shadow ever new,

And changing with the changes of the day?
Too hard I feel the task, and shrink from the essay!

In gloom, in sunshine, in the calm, the storm,
   That cliff delighted still have I survey'd :
What time the early sun hath gilt its form,
   Or midday splendour on its features play'd,
   Or evening thrown their outlines into shade;
What time against its base the wave hath plash'd,
   Serenely blue, and scarce a murmur made,
Or by the North-west wind to fury lash'd,
With billow, foam, and roar, tumultuously hath
      dash'd.

Majestic Headland! No such colonnade
   As thine can Athens or Palmyra show ;
What though by skilfull'st hands their shrines were
      made,
   And all that science, all that taste could do
   Combined with all that riches could bestow,
To make them glorious.   But no mortal hand
   Hath rear'd thy columns, PLAISKIN ! row o'er row
On thy stupendous precipice they stand,
There built, and there sustain'd by GOD's alone
      command !

1832.

A LEGEND OF THE BELLS OF
LIMERICK.[19]

Those Evening Bells, these Evening Bells,
How many a tale their music tells
Of youth, and home, and that sweet time
When last I heard their soothing chime !
MOORE.

HE wind had fallen, the sky was fair,
  Calm and mild the evening air ;
    The glorious sun,
  His day-course run,
Was setting in summer pride :
Not a murmur could be heard,
Not a single ripple stirr'd
  Against the vessel's side,
As she lay at the vesper hour,
Opposite St. Mary's Tower,
  Upon the Shannon's tide :
And the gently-dripping oar
  Sped a stranger to the shore.

A wanderer from his home was he ;
Not exiled thence by tyranny,

But that he could not bear to be
　　Where all was gone that he had loved ;
He could not bear the wreck to see
　　Of all the joys he once had proved.
In war had fallen his only son,
　　His wife beloved of grief had died,
Brothers, kindred, he had none,—
What was there now beneath the sun
　　That he could love beside ?

Yes, there was *one thing*—'twas a fond,
A foolish fancy,—yet a bond
Uniting him, by thoughts of pain,
To days he ne'er will see again.
His prime of manhood he had spent
Upon one purpose wholly bent ;
At length, the work of years complete,
　　To a holy convent he had given
A peal of bells, of tone so sweet,
　　So solemn, and so grand,
They led the thoughts perforce to heaven ;
Nor could the founder be denied
Forgiveness, if he felt some pride
　　In the work of his own hand.

They too were lost in the time of strife,
When all else was lost that he loved of life ;

The convent walls were razed to the ground,—
   The bells away were borne ;
But he fancied if their tuneful sound
   On his ear—bereft—forlorn—
Once, even once, again might play,
In peace his spirit would pass away.

The wanderer has left his own country,
He has parted in grief from fair Italy,
Many a league has he gone by sea,
      Many a mile on shore ;—
All traces of youth have pass'd away,
His form is bent, his hair is grey,
      His heart—wither'd and sore :
All Europe in vain has he travell'd round,
And he fears that much-loved tuneful sound
      He is doom'd to hear no more!
In vain has he sought : full many a time
   His breast has heaved with a bitter sigh,
As his ear has turn'd from some tuneful chime,
   Which struck no chord of his memory !

At length, by chance, a traveller tells
Of Limerick's sweet and solemn bells,
How deeply to the heart they go,
And, like religion tempering woe,
Lead up the soul from all below.

The wanderer listens to the tale,
Brightens with joy his visage pale,
   A smile is in his eye :—
" Oh! could I reach that distant Isle,
" And listen to those bells awhile,
   " Contented would I die!"

And now the bark with plashing oar
Bears the Italian towards the shore
   Across the Shannon's stream ;—
The calm and beauteous evening sky
Like his own heaven of Italy
   In its sweetest time did seem :—
On other days and scenes intent,
The wanderer's thoughts were homeward bent,
   As in a lovely dream :—
When, hark! with sweet and solemn stroke,
St. Mary's bells the stillness broke !

" Yes! they are—they are my own !"
Cried the wanderer at the tone ;
   No other word he said.
Towards the town he turn'd his face,—
A smile's faint glimmer you might trace ;
   His hands on his breast he laid :
All the joys he once had proved,—
His home—his *all that he had loved*—

All from which he had grieved to part
Came in those tones upon his heart.

Now the bark has reach'd the strand,
Now that passenger may land ;
Still upon his aged face,
  On Saint Mary's Tower fix'd,
Joy's expression you may trace,
  With a mellow'd sorrow mix'd.
But his sum of days is told,
His eyes are closed, his pulse is cold;
  In that one voice of Memory,
    On that long-hoped-for day,
  The spirit of that Wanderer
    In peace hath pass'd away!

WHAT lends the scene that wondrous
    fascination,
    Where lie the Two Lakes in the dark-
    some Glen?
Why, once beheld in silent admiration,
  Longs the rapt soul to see it once again?

'Tis not alone the charm of lake and mountain,
  Of the wild contrasts of the light and shade,
Of stream down-leaping from its hidden fountain,
  Of frowning precipice and sunny glade.

For grander scenes live in my recollection,
  And sweeter spots are in my heart enshrined;
Which, sacred to the memory of affection,
  Claim not such mighty influence o'er the mind.

'Tis not the charm of outward Nature only,
  Blending the soft, the savage, the sublime;
A spirit hovers o'er that valley lonely,
  Borne from the ruins of far-distant time.

'Tis not that royal wealth or ostentation
    In this wild scene their palaces have placed;
Nor cultured Art, nor rich Imagination
    The offerings of the pious soul have graced.

Rude in their structure, in appearance lowly,
    With nothing to attract fastidious eye,
Yet bearing tokens of their purpose holy,
    We view the relics of an age gone by.

Here Faith, and world-renouncing Veneration
    Twelve hundred years ago a seat had found,
Built shrines and homes for pious Contemplation,
    And made the narrow glen a holy ground.

How often on those peaceful homes alighted
    The invader's fury, or the civil storms;
Till, by five centuries of ruin blighted,
    There only now remain the lifeless forms.

Grand in their long-enduring desolation,
    Stamp'd with the character of days of yore;
No vain, unskill'd attempt at renovation
    Hath marr'd the features it could not restore.

Now through the Gateway's broken arch we enter,
    Our feet the precincts of the City tread;
But mark! yon Tower mysterious in the centre
    Points heavenward from a *City of the Dead!*

Beside " Our Lady's " massive doorway growing,
    The aged ivy o'er the ruin clings;
And, where the streams of Poolanass are flowing,
    The hazels flourish o'er the graves of kings!

Their histories have perish'd—idle fables
    Mingle with many a noble, holy name;
And roofless walls, and rent disfigured gables
    The honour'd title of " Cathedral " claim.

Still, 'mid the wreck, the stone-roof'd " House of
      KEVIN "
    Remains, with moss and lichen grey o'ergrown;
Still, 'mid the tombs, suggesting hopes of Heaven,
    Stands near his ruin'd church the Cross of stone.

Nations may pass, and kings and kingdoms perish,—
    Their very names forgotten from the earth;—
Yet pious gratitude the homes will cherish
    Which shelter'd first Religion's holy birth.

Dear to the soul the sight and contemplation
    Of scenes where hermits knelt, apostles trod;
Where Faith hath rear'd the symbol of Salvation,
    And humble men have sought to walk with GOD!

RADIGER.

A BALLAD OF ANGLO-SAXON HISTORY.[21]

I T was on the banks of the flowing Rhine,
    When a summer day was past,
    There sat in a tent a Ladye fair,
And her tears were flowing faſt.

Around her stood knights and mail-clad men,
    Of the high East Anglian name;
Who all to avenge that Ladye's wrong
    From merry England came.

For her sires had come, of Odin's line,
    Across the German flood,
And had won their land, by strength of hand,
    From men of British blood.

And Radiger woo'd her in early youth,
    (On Rhine's fair banks he reign'd,)
And his eagle eye, and his bearing high
    Her heart's affection gain'd.

And he pledged his faith with oath and vow,
 He pledged it with hand and glove ;
And he hasten'd afar to the fields of war,
 And she grieved not—his Ladye love ;—

But ever, when tidings of Radiger's might
 From fields well-foughten came,
Her heart beat high with joy and pride,
 To hear of her true knight's fame.

But ah ! woe worth ambition's guile,
 And man's inconstant mind !
For Radiger sought another bride,
 And his English love resign'd.

Yet he sought not that bride for her beauty's pride,
 Or the witching bloom of youth ;
But, urged by his father's stern commands,
For a wealthy widow's fertile lands,
 He broke his plighted truth.

And his true love heard of his broken faith,
 She heard of his broken vow :—
She breathed no sigh, she shed no tear,
 But she bent an angry brow.

Ill brook'd she the slight that traitor knight
 Had paid to her maiden truth ;
But she call'd to her side her brother tried,
 And the best of the Anglian youth.

" Now arm thee, now arm thee, Egfrid bold,
 " And arm thy merry-men all;
" For, before this year shall have an end,
 " False Radiger shall fall!

" I will not lye on couch of down,
 " Nor clothe me in cloke of pall,
" Till, living or dead, at my feet down laid,
 " False Radiger shall fall!"

Up then yspake her brother bold,
 He spake right brotherly;
" Now away with thy care, my sister fair,
 " For avenged thou shalt be!"

He arm'd at her call his warriors all,
 He arm'd his merry-men;
And they sail'd away at break of day,
 Six gallant ships and ten.

And when they came to the Varnian shore,
 Across the German Sea,
Young Egfrid left his sister there,
 With part of his company;

But he with the rest of his host on press'd,
 False Radiger to meet;
And he swore, unless himself were slain,
 He would bring him to her feet.

The sun has set in the western wave,
  The summer's day is past;
The moon is high in the evening sky;
  The dews are falling fast.

And the Ladye sate by the flowing Rhine,
  And wept right bitterly;
" Oh, when will my brother return and bring
  " That traitor knight to me?"

Her merry-men deem'd that Ladye wept
  Lest her brother should fall in strife;
But she fear'd not at all for Egfrid's fall,—
  She fear'd for Radiger's life.

They deem'd that she wept for his broken vow,
  That she grieved for the bitter slight;
But her grief was all lest her brother bold
  Should slay that faithless knight.

Yet still she call'd him a traitor false,
  And bent an angry brow,
As when she heard, in England fair,
  Of that traitor's broken vow.

And aye she strove to renounce her love,
  And to look with a careless eye;
But she could not restrain the falling tear,
  Nor check the deep-drawn sigh.

And though Radiger now had renounced his vow,
  And broken his plighted truth,
She could not forget the tender love
  He had won in early youth.

She knew not before that painful hour
  The strength of woman's love ;
How little the fickleness of man
  Her constancy can move.

And she sat at the door of Egfrid's tent,
  Oppress'd with thoughtful care,
And heeded not the passing hours,
  Nor felt the chilling air ;

But sudden she rose with eager start,
  And cast her eyes around,
For she heard the tread of armèd men,
  She heard the trumpet's sound :

And Egfrid return'd with his war-like host,
  All laden with foemen's spoil ;
And their dinted helms, and armour stain'd,
  Gave tokens of bloody toil :

And with trumpet sound and martial shout
  That Ladye did they greet ;
And they brought the best of the spoils they'd won,
  And laid them at her feet.

———

" Now cheer thee, my sister," Egfrid said,
  " And smooth thy ruffled brow ;
" For dearly, I trow, thy faithless foe
  " Hath paid for his broken vow !"

That Ladye's cheek was blanched, I ween,
  With the pallid hue of death ;
And painfully beat her swelling heart,
  And hardly she drew her breath.

" We have fought all day in bloody fray,
  " And many a foe is dead :
" The field was won ere set of sun ;
  " But Radiger is fled !

" We have scour'd his country far and near,
  " And done it bitter scathe ;
" And long shall Radiger rue the day
  " When he broke his plighted faith."

That Ladye's cheek, so deadly pale,
  Was flush'd with a crimson stain ;
She bent on her brother an angry brow,
  A look of high disdain.

" And is it, then, thus thou hast kept the oath
  " Thou hast sworn so gallantly,
" That thou wouldst bring that faithless knight
  " A captive to my knee ?

" And is this the price which Radiger
　　" For his broken faith must pay,—
" The paltry spoil of serfs and hinds,
　　" Which thou hast won to-day ?

" Away, then! and seek Sir Radiger,
　　" And bring him alive to me !
" For my own right hand shall deal the blow
　　" To punish his treachery !"

Sir Egfrid shrunk from her proud rebuke,
　　Her look of high disdain ;—
" Nay, calm thee, sister fair," he said,
　　" Thou shalt not ask in vain.

" My warriors brave and I will rest
　　" From warlike toil to-night ;
" But again will we go to seek thy foe
　　" With morning's early light.

" And I solemnly swear, my sister fair,
　　" I never more will thee greet,
" Until I shall bring false Radiger
　　" A captive to thy feet !"

At the break of day they rode away
　　With eager course and fast ;
But they search'd in vain both wood and plain
　　Until high noon was past.

At length they came to a forest glade,
 Where, with a chosen band,
All arm'd, I trow, from top to toe,
 Sir Radiger did stand.

" Now yield thee," cried Egfrid, " craven knight!
 " Now yield thyself to me !
" I never had thought from field of death
 " That Radiger would flee !"

" I will not yield, thou vaunting knight,
 " I will not yield to thee !
" But one of us, ere the sun shall set,
 " Slain on this field shall be.

" Stand back, stand back, my merry-men !
 " This quarrel is mine own :—
" And, Egfrid, keep thou back thine host;
 " We two must fight alone !"

Sir Egfrid he turn'd and waved his hand,
 And shouted loud and high :—
" Stand back, stand back, my merry-men ;
 " We two this fight must try !"

He clapp'd his spurs to his courser's sides,
 And charged with mortal force ;
Sir Radiger stood not the sudden shock,
 But down went man and horse.

RADIGER.

Sir Egfrid saw not his fallen foe,
    But rapidly hurried past;
Till he heard the shout his host gave out,
    Then he check'd his courser's haste.

Lightly he leapt from his courser's back,
    And lighted on the land;
Sir Radiger raised him from the ground,
    His falchion in his hand.

Now, burning with indignant shame,
    He rush'd upon his foe;
But Egfrid stood upon his guard,
    And parried the hasty blow.

Now, foot to foot, and hand to hand,
    They closed in eager strife;
But Egfrid thought of his sister's wish,
    Nor sought his foeman's life.

He saw him fight with desperate might,
    Enraged at the shameful foil;
And mark'd at length his failing strength,
    Oppress'd with fruitless toil.

Then closing fast, with hand and foot
    He twined his foeman round,
And wrench'd the falchion from his grasp,
    And bore him to the ground.

"Now, yield thee, Radiger," he cried,
  "Or certes thou must die!"
Sir Radiger turn'd aside his face,
  And heaved a bitter sigh;—

"Thou hast won the day, Sir Knight," he said,
  "I yield myself to thee!
"Thou art the first of mortal men
  "That ever conquer'd me!"

The Ladye sat in Sir Egfrid's tent,
  As closed the summer's day;
And she heard the trumpet's joyous note,
  And saw the bright array.

First of that gallant company
  She saw her brother ride,
And knew, but saw not, who was *he*
  That slowly paced beside.

"Now cheer thee, my sister," Egfrid cried,
  "My task is now complete;
"For I have brought Sir Radiger
  "A captive to thy feet!"

Sir Radiger knelt at the Ladye's feet,
  O'erwhelm'd with deep despair;—
He dared not look upon her face
  To read his sentence there.

But, " Oh, forgive!" at length he said,
  " Forgive my broken vow !
" The greatness of that heinous fault
  " I never felt till now.

" And, trust me, not for beauty's charms
  " I sought another's hand ;
" The fault was in my haughty sire,
" Who reck'd but of his vain desire
  " For lordship and for land !

" Yet, Ladye, forgive my broken vow,
  " And grant thy love again ;
" And let my future constancy
  " Wipe out my falsehood's stain !"

He said no more,—the Ladye sigh'd,
  And did all trembling stand ;
Then she look'd on the knight with a lovely smile,
And a blush crept over her cheek the while,
  As she gave her lily hand.

And Radiger left his old new bride,
  He left his fatherland,
For the English maiden's constant faith,
  And the English maiden's hand.

A ROYAL CONVERT.

HERE is a Legend of a Sclavonian Prince, whose name has passed from my memory, converted to Christianity by the sight and explanation of a picture representing the Last Judgment.

HAT mean, Old Man, these dismal sights
  of woe ?
   " And what the white-robed forms that
    float above ?
" Say, why is pain and anguish all below ?
  " Why all on high is harmony and love ?"

" Monarch ! the time shall come when all must end,
  " The world, and all that now therein appears :
" The King of kings shall from His throne descend,
  " And check the oppressor's wrong, the good
   man's tears.

" Then shall He judge in righteousness mankind,
  " By their own acts and words shall all be tried :
" The bad to lasting woe shall be consign'd,—
  " The good in bliss for ever shall abide !"

" How then, Old Man, may I escape the fire
 " That burns unceasing in that world of pain ?
" By what achievements, say, may I aspire
 " To join in realms of bliss yon white-robed
  train ? "

" Monarch, the choice is thine ! The wretches cast
 " In endless torment on yon fiery flood,
" Are they whose lives in vice and sin were past,
 " The impious, the unjust, the men of blood.

" Those white-robed bands were merciful and just,
 " Their feet the paths of holiness have trod;
" And such shall rise immortal from the dust,
 " And join eternally their King—their God ! "

" And who, Old Man, is He, of eye severe,
 " Yet full of mercy—' full of truth and grace ?'
" Fain would I strive that Being to be near—
 " To look for aye on that majestic face ! "

" Monarch ! the painter's skill in vain hath sought
 " That unseen full perfection to portray ;
" Seek thou the means which He himself hath
  wrought,
 " And thou may'st dwell with Him in bliss for aye !

F

―――――――

" Seek thou the narrow path that CHRIST hath ſhown,
    " Which will conduct thee to those courts above,
" Where thou may'st look on GOD's eternal throne,
    " Where GOD Himself is Light, and Life, and
        Love!"

MOZART'S REQUIEM.

MOZART is said to have been visited by a stranger, who requested him to compose a Requiem for the funeral of a distinguished person. He engaged to complete it in a given time; but he was in bad health: the subject greatly affected his imagination, and he became convinced that he was composing it for himself. When the appointed time came, he requested a short delay, which was granted by his unknown visitor. Mozart died on the evening the composition was completed, and the Requiem was performed at his own funeral. The stranger appeared no more.[22]

NAY, cease that flattering dream of hope!
  " Your comfort is in vain;
    " I feel my life is ebbing fast,—
  " This is my dying strain :
  " Then let me nerve my spirit's force
    " To swell each mournful tone,
  " I know this music is my last,—
    " This Requiem is *my own!*

" You say it is a fond conceit,
   " You think my fears are weak ;
" But look upon my wasted form,
   " Behold my faded cheek !
" Behold my hollow-sunken eye,
   " Its fire is nearly gone,
" Soon, soon will it be quench'd in death,—
   " This Requiem is *my own !*

" Why, but for this, each deepest charm
   " Of music have I sought?
" Why, but for this, has every power
   " Of heart and soul been wrought?
" Why, but for this, upon my work
   " Have earliest sunbeams shone,
" And midnight found me still employ'd?
   " This Requiem is *my own !*

" I knew it, from that hour when first
   " The mournful Stranger came,
" (Even then I felt the hand of Death
   " Had seized upon my frame ;)
" I read it in his tearful eye,
   " I heard it in his tone,—
" He ask'd, ' A Requiem for a friend,'—
   " I knew it was *my own.*

" Again he came—I wish'd the time
   " Prolong'd, and it was given ;

" I sought not to delay the fate
  " I knew decreed by Heaven :—
" I could not lose that favourite work
  " Till life itself was flown ;
" Even now, in death, it shall be mine,—
  " This Requiem is *my own!*

" Oh, let me then collect my strength
  " To close the solemn strain!
" Recall me not to thoughts of earth ;
  " I ne'er shall write again.
" Oh, let me pour my spirit forth
  " Before the Almighty's throne ;
" Be this, my last, my holiest work!
  " The Requiem is *my own!*"

The setting sun hath shed his beams
  Around the Minstrel's bed ;
The Dirge of Death is ended now,—
  The Author's life is fled ;
Yet, as he calmly pass'd away,
  Without one sigh or groan,
He press'd the Requiem to his heart ;—
  That Requiem *was his own!*

RAPHAEL D'URBINO.

THE strong likeness between the death of Mozart and that of Raphael, after the completion of their greatest works, was pointed out to me, after the composition of the preceding poem, many years ago, by a friend now departed, with the following quotation from Lanzi's "Storia Pittorica," in reference to Raphael's picture of the Transfiguration :—

" Questo Volta in cui adunò quanto sapea far di
" più bello e di più maestoso, fu l' estremo, e dell'
" Arte e dell' opere di Raffaello.   Da indi innanzi
" non tocco piu penelli—soppraggiunto di mortale
" infirmità si mori cristianamente nel 1520, di 37
" anni, nel Venerdi santo, ch' era stato pure il giorno
" della sua nascita : e quella gran Tavola fu esposta
" insieme col suo cadavere nella Chiesa della Ro-
" tonda."

THE Artist's task is finish'd now,
     His holiest and his last ;
With that his course of life is run,
     His wish for life is past.

Content he lays the pencil down
   He ne'er will touch again;
Content awaits the closing hour,
   Oppress'd by mortal pain.

What wonder? How could he repine,
   Or wish that hour delay'd,
Whose pencil, dipp'd in hues of heaven,
   Had such a scene portray'd;
Whose mind, from childhood's earliest years
   To holy subjects bent,
On this, most beauteous, most sublime,
   Its richest gifts had spent?

He might have lived, perchance, to feel
   His powers of mind decay,
And the rapture of triumphant Art
   Fade from his heart away;
'Twere worth a life of sorer toil,
   A death of longer pain,
In prime of life, in noon of fame,
   The bourne of rest to gain!

The Artist's work is finish'd,
   And he lays him down to die;
But the Form Divine still fills his mind,
   Still cheers his closing eye;
And the thought is thrilling in his heart,—
   " 'Tis goodly to be here,

" The Saviour's face of love to see,
  " His words of grace to hear!"

Within the fane that once enshrined
  " All Gods" of heathen Rome,
Now by a holier name inscribed
  " All Saints" of Christendom,
Beneath that vast Rotunda, mark!
  In Rome's approving view,
The Painter and his grandest work
  Are brought for honour due.

Behind the lighted altar, see!
  The glorious canvas stands,
Last enterprise of Raphael's art,
  Last work of Raphael's hands;
Before the lighted altar, hark!
  The funeral rites are said,
Where Raphael's form extended lies,
  But Raphael's soul is fled.

The Artist's work is finishèd,
  But his fame can never die;
Still glow his bright imaginings
  Where cold his ashes lie;
And the Faith that sanctified his Art,
  And nerved his parting sign,
Hath left a halo round the name
  Of " Raphael the Divine!"

COPERNICUS.

FTER thirty years of vain effort to harmonize the phenomena of the heavens with the theory of Ptolemy, which placed the earth in the centre, and made the sun, planets, and starry heavens revolve round it, Copernicus first doubted, and then disbelieved. Finally, he was convinced, by a close examination of the motions of Venus, that the sun was the centre, round which the earth and other planets revolved. But, conscious of the hazard of opposing a system defended by prejudice and by religion, he put forth his own views with great caution, and only after long delay ; and his great work, setting forth his doctrines, was never read by its author in print, and only reached him in time to cheer his dying moments.

He died in 1543, at seventy years of age, nearly an hundred years before the discoveries of Kepler and Galileo confirmed and perfected those of Copernicus.[23]

OR thirty years the patient Sage has bent
    his earnest eyes
To mark the wandering Orbs that make
    the circuit of the skies,

Has sought to trace, from year to year, the orbit of
    the Sun,
Which, since Creation, round the Earth his giant
    course has run.

For so had ancient Science taught—the Earth a
    central ball,
The Sun—the planets—moving round, on her depen-
    dent all ;
The star-besprinkled canopy, that arches o'er the
    night,
Round her revolving, hour by hour, in rapid cease-
    less flight.

" It cannot be!" the mighty doubt at length hath
    seized his mind ;
" Not thus they move in complex course, in mazes
    intertwined ;—
" Not this the grand simplicity which early students
    saw,
" Embracing all created orbs in one harmonious
    Law !"

To one fair planet now the Sage devotes his patient
    eyes,
In evening twilight marks her set, in morning twi-
    light rise,

Notes every movement, every change ;—the glorious
    truth is won,—
The centre of her course is found,—that centre is
    the Sun !

No more he doubts :—his ardent soul takes *on the
    Sun* her place :
From thence his well-stored mind surveys th' illimit-
    able space ;
Her central station Earth resigns—confusion dis-
    appears—
In beauteous order round the Sun revolve the mighty
    spheres !

But Truth is slow, and Error strong :—and scarce
    the patient Sage
Dares brave the persecution of a dark and bigot age :
With cautious words to trusted friends makes his
    discoveries known,
With cautious hand indites the truths which future
    times shall own.

There are friends around an aged man upon a humble
    bed ;
The snows of three-score years and ten are on his
    beard and head ;
Upon his noble brow and face have risen the dews
    of death ;

Yet hath his eye not lost its fire—nor lost his soul
    its faith !

Beside him lies a Holy Book ;—the path his soul
    hath trod,
'Mid heavenly orbs, hath made her cling with closer
    trust to God ;—
Beside him lies another book—unopen'd, and un-
    read,—
" Alas ! that it *too late* has come to cheer his dying
    bed !"

" Ah, no !" the patient Sage replies, " six thousand
    years have past
" Since God the glorious System framed, which I
    declare at last :
" I well may wait an hundred years till men the
    Truth shall own,
" Which He so many thousand years hath waited
    to make known !"

SACRED POEMS.

HYMN

WRITTEN FOR MUSIC.

EAR from Thine heavenly throne,
    Father of all!
Most mighty Three in One,
    Hear when we call!
Thou, who for us didst die!
    Thou, who hast made!
Thou, who dost sanctify!
    Send us Thine aid!

Hear, from Thy glorious place,
    Seated on high!
Send us, O Christ, Thy grace;
    Hear, when we cry!
By all the precious blood
    Which Thou hast pour'd,
Nail'd to the accursed wood,
    Save us, good Lord!

Save, from the deadly power
    Of our great foe !
Save, in wealth's trying hour,—
    Save us in woe !
Strengthen our humble faith,
    Built on Thy word ;
And, in the hour of death,
    Save us, good Lord !

CHRIST TRIUMPHANT.

ISAIAH, LXIII.

WHO cometh here from Edom's rocks,
 From Bozrah's haughty tower:
 That journeyeth glorious in array,
Majestic in His power?
With garments red from fields of blood,
 A Conqueror He doth seem!
" I come, who speak in righteousness,
 " The Mighty to redeem!"

And why is Thine apparel red,
 Like his who treads the vine?
And why, like his who treads the vat,
 Do all Thy garments shine?
" The winepress I have trodden out—
 " Have trodden it alone:
" And in that bloody vintage-hour
 " With Me there stood not one.

" In anger did I trample them,
 " In fury did I tread;

G

" Their blood is sprinkled on My robe,
   " My raiment all is red :
" The awful day is in Mine heart
   " Of vengeance on My foes ;
" The year is come when I redeem
   " My people from their foes.

" And I beheld—but none could save
   " His brethren by his hand ;
" I wondering saw no child of man
   " In that dread day could stand ;—
" Therefore Mine own right arm alone
   " My great salvation brought ;
" And by my strength of zeal upheld
   " The conquest I have wrought!"

Yes ! Thou hast conquer'd mightier foes
   Than Edom's hostile power,
Hast Victor come from stronger holds
   Than Bozrah's haughty tower !
For Thou hast burst the gates of Death,
   And laid beneath Thee low,
By Thy right hand and holy arm,
   Thine Israel's hellish foe !

Thou didst behold no child of man
   His brother's soul could save,
Or make agreement unto GOD
   To free him from the grave ;

A costlier price their souls demand
　Than man hath power to pay;
And therefore Thou, O Christ, wouldst die
　That we might live for aye!

And therefore, when the appointed year
　Of Thy redeemèd came,
Thou didst assume the flesh of man,
　Didst take a mortal frame;
Thou didst the bloody winepress tread
　Of suffering from Thy foes,
To save Thy people from their sins,
　From hell's eternal woes.

And therefore, when o'er Hell and Death
　The conquest Thou hadst won,
Thou didst ascend to GOD's right hand,
　And take Thy glorious throne;
There still dost thou retain, O Lord,
　The Mediator's seat,
Until the LORD shall make Thy foes
　The footstool for Thy feet.

Gird then, O Thou most mighty One,
　Thy sword upon Thy thigh!
Ride forth! Avenge Thee on Thy foes
　Who still Thy Name defy!

But when that winepress of Gᴏᴅ's wrath
Thy conquering feet shall tread,
Help us, Thy children, Lord, for whom
Thy precious blood was shed !

Thou art our Father,—though not us
Hath Abraham begot ;—
Though Isaac, and though Israel
Our names acknowledge not !
Thou art our Father still, O Christ,
And our Redeeming Lord,
The Righteousness of Gᴏᴅ most high,
The One Eternal Word !

A LITANY TO THE HOLY SPIRIT.

(IMITATED FROM HERRICK.)[24]

I.

OLY Spirit! Gift of Heaven,
By the Saviour's promise given
To the heart by sorrow riven;
Sweet Spirit, comfort me!

Spirit Thou of Love and Peace!
Give my weary heart release,—
Bid its sinful struggles cease :—
Sweet Spirit, comfort me!

Spirit Thou of meek enduring,
With Thy strength our weakness curing,
And with holy Hope assuring,—
Sweet Spirit, comfort me!

II.

WHEN I go, from morn to night,
Toiling in the Christian fight,
Needing strength, and needing light,
Sweet Spirit, comfort me!

When the road seems steep and strait,
And I feel my labour great,
Bending with my burden's weight,
  Sweet Spirit, comfort me!

When the toil my spirit paineth;—
When each effort vainly straineth,
Nor the mark appointed gaineth:—
  Sweet Spirit, comfort me!

III.

WHEN the cares of mortal life,
Round my pathway gathering rife,
Bar me in the Christian strife,
  Sweet Spirit, comfort me!

When my way is dark and drear,
And mine eyesight is not clear;
When I need a voice to cheer;
  Sweet Spirit, comfort me!

When my heart within me quaileth
For the trouble that assaileth;
When the friend I've trusted faileth,
  Sweet Spirit, comfort me!

IV.

WHEN my soul is sick with sin
And the taint that is within;
When I fain would pardon win;
  Sweet Spirit, comfort me!

When I muse on Him who died
With His pierced hands and side;
Trusting on the Crucified;
  Sweet Spirit, comfort me!

When I make my sad confession,
Through His heavenly intercession
Pleading still for man's transgression,
  Sweet Spirit, comfort me!

V.

WHEN my prayer is faint and weak;—
When I know not what to seek;—
In the sighs that cannot speak,
  Sweet Spirit, comfort me!

In the time of rest and ease,
When the snares of wealth increase;—
Thou, whose chastening touch is peace,
  Sweet Spirit, comfort me!

In the days of tribulation,
In the hours of deep vexation,
When from sorrow comes temptation,
　Sweet Spirit, comfort me!

VI.

WHEN the shade is o'er me cast;
When life's light is fading fast;
In the hour of death, at last,
　Sweet Spirit, comfort me!

By the blood of GOD's dear Son
Cleanse my soul from evil done;
And by faith in Him alone,
　Sweet Spirit, comfort me!

On the morn of Resurrection,
By His blood and Thy protection,
With assurance of perfection,
　Sweet Spirit, comfort me!

THE DAILY SERVICE OF GOD'S CHURCH.

WHEN in the desert forty years
    The tribes of God abode,
  And o'er their camp His glorious cloud
  The Almighty's presence show'd;
Each morn and eve from Aaron's hands
  Behold the incense rise;
Each morn and eve his people bring
  The appointed sacrifice.

Such was their service, when at length
  The promised rest they gain'd,
In Shiloh while the curtain'd tent
  The Ark of God contain'd;
Each morn and eve the lamb was slain,
  Type of the Lamb Divine;
Each morn and eve the Type of Prayer
  Burn'd in the Holy Shrine.

Such, when the house, by David plann'd,
  Was built by David's son,
And in the Temple's holiest place
  Jehovah's glory shone;

Each morn and eve the Priests in course
   Were wont their part to bear ;
Each morn and eve the people came
   For daily praise and prayer.

Here Simeon, waiting for the LORD,
   Devoutly would resort,
And aged Anna day nor night
   Forsook that holy court ;
And here their longing eyes beheld
   SALVATION's dawning ray,
The " Glory of His Israel's race,
   " The Gentiles' opening day."

What though, when Christ had died and risen,
   No lamb need suffer there,
Still John and Peter sought its gates
   At wonted " Hour of Prayer :"
Still in those courts, " with one accord,
   " The faithful daily stay'd,"
And daily broke, " from house to house,
   " The consecrated bread."

So, when at length His Church had pass'd
   Her persecution-fires,
When Queens her nursing-mothers were,
   And Kings her nursing-sires ;

Where'er for worship of her Lord
  The stately shrine was raised,
There, morn and eve, " the prayer was made,
  " And daily was He praised."

So, when our Island Church was cleansed
  From superstition's stain,
And offer'd, as in earliest times,
  Unsullied rites again,
She fail'd not to instruct her sons
  To " praise Him day by day,"
Each morn and eve to hear His Word,
  Each morn and eve to pray.

What though neglect and worldly cares
  Have chill'd devotion's flame,
His daily mercies and *our* wants
  A daily homage claim ;
Still day by day the praise is due
  To Him who guards our bed,
Still day by day we need the prayer
  That asks " our daily bread."

How good in God's own house each day
  Our errors to confess ;
Each day to hear His Word of peace,
  Of truth, of righteousness ;

Each day in common Psalms and Hymns
   Our grateful part to bear;
And, for our own and others' wants,
   To join in Common Prayer!

And so our Zion's holiest sons
   Have loved to seek the shrine,
When summon'd by the daily bell
   To offices divine;
Have joy'd to feel their praise and prayer
   Like morning incense rise,
Their lifting up of holy hands
   Like evening sacrifice!

POEMS OF SENTIMENT AND

IMAGINATION.

LAYS OF THE SEASONS.

SUMMER LONGINGS.

(FOR MUSIC.)

 WOULD I were in the greenwood
      bowers,
  In the lone and lovely vale,
Where odours of the summer flowers
  Are floating on the gale ;
Where fields are green, and 'mid the woods
  The birds are singing free,—
Where murmuring flow the mountain floods,
  For there's the home for me !

I'd leave the city's lofty towers,
  Its crowds and dazzling glare,
To hear the birds, to cull the flowers,
  To breathe the mountain air !

There are slaves within the halls of pride,
The fields—the woods are free!
I would I were by the greenwood side,
For there's the home for me!

SUMMER EVENING MUSINGS.

WHEN eve is gently stealing on,
    O'er mountain, wood, and hill,
    The heart of meditative mood
What holy musings fill !
How does each sight direct the soul
    From earth to Heaven to look,
And read the praise of Nature's God
    In Nature's lovely book!

Behold the lilies clothed by Him !
    Less glorious far than they
The greatest king that ever reign'd
    In all his bright array :
Observe the birds ! His praise they sing,
    To Him in want they flee ;—
Will He who clothes the flower, the bird,
    Deny His care to thee ?

The cattle seek their home, and claim
    Their master's wonted care,

H

To ease them from their daily toil,
    And needful food prepare :—
Trust thou in Him who shall thy soul
    In heavenly pastures feed,
And to the waters of His grace
    Thy weary spirit lead !

The sun, who as a giant rose,
    Rejoicing in his might,
Is yielding to the gentler moon,
    The ruler of the night,
And, gilding with his parting rays
    The chambers of the West,
With promise of a glorious morn
    Is sinking to his rest.

So may I strive, whate'er my lot,
    To do my Maker's will,
And still, from day to day, with joy
    My duty's course fulfil ;
That when my sun at length shall set,
    And life shall pass away,
The night of death may only lead
    To everlasting day !

THE FALL OF THE LEAF.

(WRITTEN FOR MUSIC.)

NAY, seek not now to check my grief,
    " I wish not to be gay,—
    " For tears alone can bring relief
    " For what I feel to-day!
" The wind is blowing loud and shrill,—
    " The leaves are falling brown and sere,—
" Each flower that dies upon the hill
    " Tells of the dying year!

" How many, in this year's short round,
    " The lovely and the brave,
" Have fallen, like leaves, upon the ground,—
    " Are slumbering in the grave!
" How soon may we be like the leaf
    " That left its parent stem to-day!
" Then let me seek in tears relief,—
    " I could not now be gay!"

Nay, check thy tears! the flower that dies
    Will blossom yet again,

When Winter's storms have left the skies,
  And Spring renews the plain ;—
And so the hour that takes thy breath
  More lasting, brighter joys shall bring ;—
A glorious Life shall rise from Death—
  An everlasting Spring !

DARK DAYS.

(WRITTEN FOR MUSIC.)

NO—in vain to hide my sorrow
    I assume a cheerful smile ;
    And the mask of gladness borrow,
Though my heart is sad the while :

For the stream, in silence gliding,
    Deepest and most darkly flows ;—
And the heart, in secret hiding,
    Feels with sharpest pang its woes !

Let me then indulge my sorrow,—
    Vain the effort to be gay ;—
Brighter hopes may dawn to-morrow,—
    All is dark and sad to-day !

I have hoped, when hope was madness—
    I have lived to see it vain !
Yet in hours of deepest sadness
    Still I cling to hope again !

For the Spring's most lovely flowers
　　Rise from Winter's chilling night;—
And the storm that blackest lowers
　　Yields before the sunbeam's light.

Thus perchance the clouds of sadness
　　From my brow may pass away,
And again the smile of gladness
　　Gild the brow so sad to-day!

WINTER CONSOLATIONS.

(WRITTEN FOR MUSIC.)

EEP not, weep not for the hours
    Of sunshine that are past!
   Though the wintry wind is blowing
      cold,
And the leaves are falling fast;
The prospect yet shall brighter grow,
    And sweeter flowers will bloom;—
Weep not, weep not! though to-day
    The sky is hung with gloom.

Weep not, weep not! though the hopes,
    That lately seem'd so sweet,
Have vanish'd like the dreams of morn,
    As baseless and as fleet ;
For other hopes more true will rise,
    And life be bright again;—
Weep not, weep not! though to-day
    Thy path be mark'd with pain!

Weep not, weep not! when the clouds,
    That now so dark appear,

Shall melt before the bursting sun,
And heaven again be clear ;
How slight to memory then will seem
The storms that saddest lower !
Weep not, weep not for the grief
That may but last an hour !

SPRING REJOICINGS.

THE Spring! The Spring! I dearly love
  The happy joyous Spring!
 When the primrose bud is bursting forth,
  And the lark begins to sing;
When the little birds are building in
  Each bank, and bush, and tree;
And waken'd from its death-like sleep
  All nature seems to be.

Oh, the Summer it is lovely, when
  The rose her sweetness yields;
And the Autumn time is gladsome too
  When harvest crowns the fields;
And happy is the Winter's hearth,
  And merry is its cheer;
But best of all I love the Spring,
  The morning of the year!

I love to tread the elastic sod
  When the herbage springs again,
And o'er the furrow'd ground to see
  The farmer sow the grain;

But, best of all, from the opening bud
　　The tender leaves to see,
And, best of all, to hear aloft
　　The lark's sweet melody !

The Spring ! The Spring ! I dearly love
　　The happy joyous Spring !
Then heavenward rise the buoyant thoughts
　　Like lark upon the wing,
Forgetful of the troubled scenes
　　That throng this world of care,
And fix'd upon the perfect joys
　　That shall be endless there.

The Heathen sorrow'd that " the flowers,[25]
　　" Which had in Autumn died,
" Again reviving, court the Spring,
　　" And bloom in Summer pride ;
" But men, the great, the strong, the wise,
　　" When comes our hour of doom,
" Sleep sound within the hollow'd earth
　　" In endless, wakeless gloom."

Not such the Christian's happier Hope ;—
　　The flower he sees revive[26]
Reminds him of that heavenly Spring
　　When he again shall live ;

When that which, " in corruption sown,"
   Hath moulder'd to decay,
Shall rise to never-fading bloom,
   In one eternal day !

CONSUMPTION.

'TIS sad to see when early nipp'd the bud
  of childhood lies,—
    'Tis sad when, fallen in prime of strength,
    the flower of manhood dies,—
'Tis sad, when age is wearied out, when manhood's
    strength is past,
And in " the sere and yellow leaf" sinks down to
    rest at last ;

But nought so sad as to behold in youth's most
    blooming day
The wasting sickness seize the frame, and wear the
    strength away;
When Medicine can only sigh, and own her aid is
    vain ;
And still the victim bears the pang, yet never will
    complain !   .

When the hectic flush upon the cheek supplants the
    bloom of health,
Yet nought declares the pain except the sigh escaped
    by stealth ;—

But saddest is the deep-drawn cough that racks the
    wasted breast,
While the languid eye too truly tells the sufferer
    cannot rest !

Yet no thought is there of self, but all of those
    who're left behind ;
And still, the weaker grows the frame, the stronger
    seems the mind :—
For, with each pang the body feels, new strength
    from high is given,
And the trial of the mortal part but fits the soul for
    Heaven !

YESTERDAY.

'TIS gone! we never can recall
    The moments pass'd away:
And memory—memory now is all
    We have of yesterday!

Our memory sadly loves to dwell
    On ills of yesterday,—
Our hopes are of to-morrow's good,—
    We never live to-day!

Vain hopes! that morrow, so desired,
    Is ever far away:—
Vain memory! no regrets can change
    One ill of yesterday!

A few short moments more of pains
    And joys must pass away;
And all our morrows here on earth
    Will be with yesterday!

ON MOURNFUL MUSIC.

"' I am never merry when I hear sweet music.''

" Perhaps," says the king Dushmanta, in the Hindû drama
of Sacontala, " the sadness of men, otherwise happy, on seeing
" beautiful forms and listening to sweet melody, arises from
" some faint remembrance of past joys, and the traces of con-
" nections in a former state of existence.''

MAURICE, *Hindû Antiq*.

H, why are happy hearts and gay
  By Music led to thoughts of sorrow ?
 Why love from pensive strain or lay
A chasten'd sadder tone to borrow ?

Why is it, when the day is past
 In every change of joyous gladness,
We love the calm that breathes at last
 From Music's thrilling tone of sadness ?

As when a stormy day is o'er,
 And now the tempest's roar is dying,
'Tis sweet to wander on the shore,
 And hear its murmurs faintly sighing !

Is it that while upon the ear
  The mournful strains are softly stealing,
Their sound recalls some scene most dear,
  And strikes some hidden chord of feeling?

Then, while we listen to each tone,
  Forgetting all the joys before us,
Visions of pleasure past and gone
  In fancy's eye come crowding o'er us!

Perhaps it may be that the soul,
  An exile from her native heaven,
Feels, as the tones of music roll,
  Traces of joys that there were given :—

Faint traces! which at times return,
  Although the brighter joys are vanish'd,
While in the bosom dimly burn
  Gleams of the Heaven from which 'tis banish'd.

Thus, while the sweetest notes recall
  Thoughts of that bliss surpassing measure,
The Soul, still mindful of her fall,
  Feels human grief obscure her pleasure!

MUSIC IN SADNESS.

(WRITTEN FOR MUSIC.)

RISE! rise! Minstrel, arise!
   Strike thy soft harp in its mournfullest
      strains!
   Strike! for no balm
   My spirit can calm
Like the deep feeling thy music contains!
   Strike! for my breast
   With grief is opprest,
Which must swell into madness, or melt into tears;
   Soon from my soul
   The shadows will roll,
When the soft voice of music descends on my ears!

   Nay! nay! Sing not to-day
Aught that is merry or joyous to me!
   Useless and vain
   That livelier strain;—
Mournful and sad should the melody be!
   Seek not to force
   My grief from its course,—

Let the full bitter tide of my sorrow flow on!
      I may listen again
      To a happier strain,
When my heart is relieved—when its shadows are
    gone!

PARTING.

(WRITTEN FOR MUSIC.)

HY should we yield to reflections of
      sorrow?
    In looks be we merry, although not
      in heart :—
Time to be sad will be left us to-morrow,—
    Why should we sadden to-day ere we part?

Why, over future afflictions lamenting,
    Lose the few moments we yet may enjoy?
Why, for the ills that are now past preventing,
    Moments so precious with sadness alloy?

No! let us strive to enjoy the last minute
    Which Time, rolling rapidly onward, will give ;
And drain Pleasure's cup of the last drop that's in it,—
    Memory will sweeten that drop while we live!

No! let us hope for a happier meeting,—
    While our hearts are as warm, and our eyes are
      as gay!
The kind voice of welcome, the glad smile of greeting,
    Will drown all the pain of our parting to-day!

FOREBODINGS.

" When shall we Six meet again ?" [27]

LAS! dear friends, the poet's song of
       cheer
      Was the faint breathing of a sadden'd
      heart;
The hour that severs us is all too near,—
   Too deep the feeling *what it is to part.*

For in this world of change the word " Farewell"
   May scarce be said without a thrill of pain :—
And, after days so happy, who can tell
   If we, who part, shall ever meet again?

How blithely sail'd we on the sunny wave,
   How gaily climb'd the steep and craggy hill,
Together rested in the mountain cave, .
   Or sought the course of the sequester'd rill !

Ours has been all that could an hour beguile,
   The charms of poesy, the game of mirth ;
Ours, too, has been the merry laugh and smile,
   To which the heart's own gaiety gave birth.

And every day has been so free from care,
   That, which the sweetest, scarcely can we say ;
But all must end :—and who can say if e'er
   We meet again, so many, and so gay ?

For some may wander under distant skies,
   Lands may divide, and seas between us roll ;
The cares and griefs of life too soon will rise,
   And check " the genial current of the soul."

Or soon each thought and feeling may be changed,
   Some fancied wrong our memories may blot ;
And we may meet again, with hearts estranged,
   Each happy moment—each kind word—forgot !

O ! thought of all most sad and full of pain !
   Better to know our lots far distant cast,
Yet vainly hope that we may meet again,—
   Than meet, *forgetful* of these pleasures past !

For who, that has a soul, could bear to part
   From hearts so kind, and eyes so joyous *now*,
And meet instead the *worse than stranger* heart,—
   The half-averted eye—the clouded brow ?

Yet such may be our lot,—for such has been,
   Ere now, the lot of other hearts as gay,
Whose fancy, changing with each changing scene,
   To-morrow leaves no memory of to-day.

But hence, such sad Forebodings! and again
   Hope we to meet, with feelings unestranged,
With cloudless memory, with no thought of pain,
   In age, in minds advanced, in hearts unchanged!

For *me*, remembrance of each happy hour
   Shall each delight enhance, and soothe each ill;
Sweet, e'en at distance, like that favourite flower,
   Whose leaves, though faded, keep some sweetness
       still!

1828.

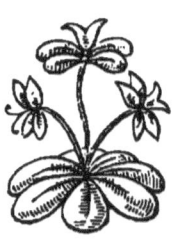

RETROSPECT.

TO MY SISTER.

TURN we, Sister, back our glances,—
    Were the sad forebodings vain?
    Were they only sickly fancies?
No! the Six ne'er met again!

Of so many kindly-hearted,
    Some were sever'd—once for aye;
Some have rarely met, and parted,
    Passing on life's busy way.

No unkindness e'er estranged us;
    Friendly memories still remain;
Time hath only slowly changed us;
    But the Six ne'er met again!

Soon the cares of life have found us
    Each within a separate sphere;
And the friendly ties that bound us
    Yield to bonds more close and dear.

Two their hearts for life have plighted,—
  Mine the joy, and mine the pain,—
Death that bond has disunited,—
  Six can never meet again!

Sweet those days of happy greetings,—
  Dear the pleasures which they gave,—
But the partings and the meetings
  All are now beyond the grave.

Still their memory may be cherish'd,
  And, where souls immortal reign,
When the dreams of life have perish'd,
  Still we all may meet again!

1845.

H, say not life has not a joy
    For those it takes away,
      Though " the glow of early thought
          decline,"
    And passion's warmth decay ;
Though with the spring-tide of the soul
    Its wilder joys be past,
And, deepening o'er the stream of life,
    The shades of care be cast.

Though the lightsome eye and cloudless brow
    Of youth be fled and gone,
Say, does the happiness of man
    Depend on *these* alone ?
Hast thou no " magnet of thy course "
    To guide thee to the shore,
Where tears shall from all eyes be dried,
    And sorrow be no more ?

Though commerce with an evil world
    Thine heart hath stricken cold,

And though the fount of tears be stopp'd
  That freely flow'd of old;
A ray from Heaven e'en yet may warm
  With life that heart of stone,
And others' woes may force the tear
  That falls not for thine own!

In vain thou seek'st the halls of mirth
  And laughter's maddening sound,
Can grief that inly racks the soul
  By revelry be drown'd?
Oh, fly for comfort to the hopes
  Of brighter joys above,—
To the heavenly mercy of thy God,
  His pity, and His love!

And though thy sorrow here on earth
  No comfort may receive,
Yet may thy soothing hand perchance
  Another's woes relieve;
As the palm-tree, in the desert, shades
  The way-worn traveller's brow,
Though on itself unshaded falls
  The sun's meridian glow.

A WISH AT EVENING.

OH, could I leave this dull cold earth,
    " And reach some fairy bowers,
    " And wander in a land unknown
" Of ' music, light, and flowers ;'
" Just such a land, methinks, might lie
    " Beyond yon golden cloud,
" Far from the busy troubled world,
    " The selfish, and the proud !

" Oh, there, untouch'd by mortal cares,
    " And bathed in heavenly light,
" The soul in freedom might enjoy
    " Her native, pure delight ;
" Where sweetest sounds should charm the ear,
    " And flowers eternal bloom ;
" No grief should enter there—no dread
    " Of sickness and the tomb !

" But here, alas, the soul is bound
    " By ties of mortal pain ;
" In vain, a *prisoner* to the earth,
    " She strives to burst her chain !

" Yes! she is of immortal birth,
    " And seeks a home divine ;
" Oh, wherefore in this troubled world
    " Is she condemn'd to pine ?"

'Tis true, fair mourner, that the soul
    Is not of mortal birth,
But wanders toward a distant home,
    A *pilgrim* upon earth ;
Yet though she lingers in the land
    Of fancy's fairy dreams,
Not *such* may be her place of rest,
    All lovely though it seems !

No ear of man hath ever heard,
    No eye hath ever seen,
The heart of man may not conceive,
    The glories of that scene,
Where she may rest at length in peace,—
    Thus much to know is given,
She has indeed a home divine,—
    Her resting-place is Heaven !

THE SPIRIT OF BEAUTY,

REPRESENTED AS A LOVELY CHILD SEATED IN A ROSE.

" Beauty shines forth in all His works in symmetry and
order."—*Lecture on Wisdom, Strength, and Beauty.*

HAT beautiful form are yon rose-leaves
      disclosing?
    What sylph has made choice of so
      lovely a bed?
'Tis the Spirit of Beauty in sweetness reposing—
   That Spirit whose power through all Nature is
     shed!

'Twas she, when the dawn of Creation was springing,
   Attended the work of the " Ancient of days,"
When the stars of the morning with gladness were
     singing,
   And the sons of the Highest were shouting His
     praise!

When the Sun first appear'd, his full brightness
     revealing,
   She illumined the sky with his orient light;

When first over Nature the evening was stealing,
　　She soften'd the rays of the Planet of night.

And thus, from the Sun in his glorious station,
　　To the planets that round him unceasingly roll,
The Spirit of Beauty pervades the Creation,
　　Uniting in exquisite order the whole :

And filling each part of the System of Nature,
　　From the orb of a sun to the bell of a flower,
Still she tends to the glory of one great Creator,
　　Exalting His wisdom, adorning His power!

HELVELLYN.

 STOOD on the top of the mighty HEL-
    VELLYN;
        Beneath me a Tarn in its mossy bed
        lay,
From whose basin unruffled a streamlet, forth
    welling,
        Pursued through the Vale of GLENRIDDING its way.
And ULLESWATER's length was extended before me,
    Begirt with its mountain-banks rugged and wild,
As blue as the sky that hung cloudlessly o'er me,
    As peaceful and calm as the sleep of a child.

Around me the features of Nature were lying,
    In sternest and awfullest grandeur outspread;
And my eye roved enraptured, each mountain des-
        crying
        Which raised o'er the valley its cloud-shadow'd
        head.
There SKIDDAW its cone to the sky was uprearing,
    Which proudly looks down over DERWENT's clear
        Lake;
There, BORROWDALE's Valley was darkly appearing;
    There, rose over LANGDALE the pass of the STAKE.

There, GRASSMOOR, the prospect more distantly
    crowning,
  O'er CRUMMOCK's deep waters hung far in the
    west ;
There, the PILLAR's high precipice, awfully frowning,
  Exalted o'er Ennerdale's LIZA his crest.
Here PIKES, and here SCA-FELL, his rival and brother,
  Whose summits a deep rocky fissure divides,
Scowling grimly across it, as hating each other,
  Look'd scornfully down on all mountains besides. [29]

And further in distance, more southward advancing,
  Old CONISTON's mountain his pinnacle raised ;
While, near me, each streamlet in sunlight was
    glancing
  In its deep rocky chasm, as delighted I gazed.
With transport I hail'd every tarn-springing fountain,
  Which foamingly rush'd down the hill's rugged
    side ;
With transport I hail'd every cliff, every mountain,
  Which the heather's rich blossom with purple
    had dyed.

I had wander'd among them—had noted each feature,
  In sunshine and shadow, in smile and in tears ;
And the memory of these, the deep secrets of Nature,
  Shall yield not to sorrow, shall fade not in years !

I had wander'd among them—had felt the wild
    pleasure
Their free-sweeping breezes can give to the heart:—
Had felt that *wealth* had not so precious a treasure,
Ambition no rapture so pure could impart!

O! dearer to me are the airs of the mountain,
    As aloft on their health-bearing courses they blow;
And sweeter, far sweeter, the gush of the fountain,
    As it bursts from its rock to the streamlet below!
And I would not exchange one such hour that I've
    wander'd,
    As wild as the star-grass that blooms on the ground,
For years that in heartless amusements are squander'd,
    By the votaries whom Fashion in fetters has bound.

They know not, who live in such slavish devotion,
    When vanity's schemes their best feelings alloy,—
They know not the deep, the heart-thrilling emotion
    Which Nature's admirer alone can enjoy;
While thus, in the wildest retreats of Creation,
    He looks up with faith to their Author above,
Who hath placed the round world on its solid
    foundation,
    Which He made by His power, and adorns in
        His love!

H ! pleasant in the woodland is
    The cooing of the Dove,
    And the evensong of Nightingales
  Is lovely in the grove,
And sweetly sings his matin song
  The Thrush on tree-top high ;
But dearest far to me the Lark,
  That singeth in the sky !

The earth-brown bird upriseth from
  His nest upon the ground,
And with his thrilling song of joy
  Fills all the air around ;
It seems as Earth had sent him forth
  To sound her Maker's praise,
To thank Him for returning Spring,
  And hopes of Summer days.   ·

High poised above the fertile field,
  He warbles, clear and high,
And sings the charms of early dawn
  When sunrise gilds the sky,

And the gladsome springing of the flowers;
   And, circling yet above,
In softer, sweeter notes proclaims
   The joys of early love!

Still rises the unwearied bird;
   Yet, though beyond the sight,
The ear can catch the distant notes
   Which quiver with delight,
Which speak the rapture of a heart
   O'erflowing with its glee,
With fervent longings after light,
   And Heaven, and liberty!

Yet longer could I listen, for
   So lovely is the strain!
But, see, the Lark, exhausted now,
   Drops down to earth again :—
For all too weak his mortal wings
   That heavenward flight to bear,
And all too gross his earthly breast
   To breathe that heavenly air!

Yet, *not in vain*,—though earth recalls
   The dust that earth hath given,—
The Lark hath spread his soaring wing,
   And drunk the air of Heaven;

In search of light and liberty,
  From earth's delights he sprung;
And light and liberty to earth
  His rapturous notes have sung!

And so the high-aspiring soul,
  That fain would heavenward rise,
Returneth oft, with strength o'ertask'd,
  Recall'd by earthly ties;
Returneth, but with heart refresh'd
  To meet each earthly care,
With hopes of light and liberty,
  That breathe in heavenly air!

THE FOG-BELLS.

1.

T IS midnight! On the margin of the wide-
extended Strand
The tide is ebbing gently from the
shallow shelving sand :
The crescent moon an hour ago hath sunk beneath
the sky ;
There is no cloud ; and yet no light of stars hath
reach'd the eye.

At either horn of that wide bay its form a lighthouse
rears,[31]
To guide the seaman in his course, as to the shore
he steers ;
When sets the sun each light must burn, till dawns
again the morn,
From rock, from breaker, and from shoal the mariner
to warn.

One, on a steep and rocky point, beneath the dark
hill side,
With steady ray, from dangerous cliffs the helms-
man's eye may guide ;

The other, with alternate gleam, now burns with
      ruby glow,
Now shines with clear and argent beam the harbour's
      mouth to show.

And where, beside the long sea-wall flows down the
      River's course,
And where the broad and sandy bar provokes the
      breaker's force ;
There, in mid centre of the Bay, a third the billow
      braves,
A giant, with a crown of fire, upstanding in the
      waves.

So, in the voyage of our life, the LORD His lights
      doth place,
The cheering beacon of His Word, the presence of
      His grace ;
To warn from rocks and shoals of sin, to stem
      temptation's force,
And to the haven of His rest to guide our wander-
      ing course.

II.

'TIS midnight! Not a cloud in heaven above
    the silent strand!
But murky fog, like funeral pall, hangs
    over sea and land;
The seaman's eye in vain may seek the cheering
    beacon light,
Nor ruby glow, nor argent beam may pierce the
    gloom to-night!

But the deep stillness of the night is broken by a
    BELL,
Which in that thick funereal gloom sounds like a
    funeral knell!
And hark! the harbour watchman gives not the
    sound alone,—
The watcher on the rocky point responds the mourn-
    ful tone!

And so, throughout the gloom, one bell still answereth
    to the other,
As brother in the hour of woe responds the sigh of
    brother :—

Across the silent midnight air how solemnly they
  toll,
As if to say, " In mercy pray for each endanger'd
  soul!"

And yet, not such their meaning ;—but when mist
  obscures the sight,
Nor through the murky fog can pierce the beacon's
  wonted light,
From rocky point and harbour pier the deep-toned
  Fog-bells toll,
To tell the entrance of the port, to warn from rock
  and shoal.

And, when the light of GOD's own Word hath fail'd
  to pierce the gloom,
Through which the sinner blindly is hurrying to his
  doom ;
The sound, of woe and death that tells, in mercy
  oft is given,
And the soul is warn'd, by funeral knells, where lies
  the course to Heaven !

CLOUDS AND SUNSHINE.

" The clouds which intercept the heavens, come not from heaven, but from the earth."—W. S. LANDOR.

HOW bright this morning rose the sun,
    The sky how clear and fair!
    The promise of a glorious day
  Was in the balmy air!
To soon, alas! the promise fades,
  The clouds obscure the skies,—
But the clouds, that hide the view of heaven,
  From earth, not heaven, arise.

The sun, that early shone so bright,
  Exhaled the morning dew ;
From hill, and marsh, and meadow-land,
  The moisture upward flew :
By winds in masses gather'd
  The clouds o'erspread the skies ;
But the clouds, that hide the view of heaven,
  From earth, not heaven, arise.

They gather dark and darker round,
  Until at length again
The bursting clouds discharge their load
  In heavy tears of rain :

While lasts that storm, no cheering beam
   May reach the longing eyes;
But the clouds, that hide the view of heaven,
   From earth, not heaven, arise.

But lo! upon that darksome veil
   A wondrous light appears!
The rainbow, 'mid the falling shower,
   Its arch of promise rears!
That bow of hope is tinted by
   A glory from the skies;—
But the clouds, that hide the view of heaven,
   From earth, not heaven, arise.

And now the clouds are breaking off,
   And, where the sun should shine,
The shroud, that still obscures his face,
   His beams with silver line:
That " silver lining of the cloud"
   Is borrow'd from the skies,—
But the clouds, that hide the view of heaven,
   From earth, not heaven, arise.

So, in the morning of our life,
   When all is bright and gay,—
When promise of untroubled joy
   Is in the early day;

The heavenward prospect, clear and fair,
　　Seems open to our eyes;
Till clouds, that hide the view of heaven,
　　From earth, not heaven, arise.

From earthly passions, fraught with sin,
　　Those vapours have their birth,—
From warm affections, roused too soon,—
　　From sorrows of the earth;
No more the upward prospect now
　　Looks clear to hopeful eyes;
But the clouds, that hide the view of heaven,
　　From earth, not heaven, arise.

Nor will that view grow clear, until
　　The heart shall find relief;—
Then let the tears unchidden fall,
　　That flow for human grief;
Nor check the penitential shower,
　　Which God will not despise,
From clouds, that hiding heavenly light,
　　From earth, not heaven, arise.

For on those showers, which earth claims back
　　From earthly sin or woe,
A solemn gleam of light from heaven
　　Shines like the tinted bow:

The clouds, that hide the view of heaven,
From earth, not heaven, arise ;—
But toward the earth from heaven the beam
Of peace and pardon flies!

And though some clouds, not yet dispersed,
May hang around our way,
The Sun of Righteousness shall gild
Their skirts with cheering ray:
The clouds, that shroud the heavens awhile,
From earth, not heaven, arise;
But the light, that *dwells behind the gloom*,
Is Light that *never dies!*

FTER months of weary leisure,
  Home and toil I sought again :
  Much I found that gave me pleasure,
Much I miss'd that caused me pain.

To my garden forth I wander'd,
  Spot with sweetest memories fraught ;
Past delights in heart I ponder'd,
  Mix'd with many an anxious thought.

There no spoiler's hand had ventured,
  Of its beauties to bereave ;
But, unwatch'd, neglect had enter'd,
  And its wildness made me grieve.

For the earth, that bears the flower,
  Bears the bramble and the weed ;
And each plot, and path, and bower,
  Of a busy hand had need.

Now the winter storms were ended ;
  Spring resumed her welcome reign ;
And the garden, long untended,
  Claim'd each leisure hour again.

Where the brightest shrubs were blowing,
  Thickest there the Bramble grew ;—
And the rankest weeds were growing
  Where the Roses ever blew ;

And the Myrtle, slowly pining,
  Wither'd in its sunny place,
Where the serpent Bindweed twining,
  Wrapt it in too close embrace ;

And the honey'd Woodbine clinging
  O'er the Lilac rear'd its head ;
And the sweetest flowers were springing—
  Straying wild o'er path and bed.

Then, while hand and knife applying,
  Where each plant and flower had need,—
Pruning some, and others tying,—
  Rooting out the baneful weed ;

In my garden as I wander'd,
  Busy with the peaceful toil,
Much within my heart I ponder'd
  Lessons rising from the soil.

Thorns and briers are the token
  Of our Sire's primeval sin,
Signs of God's commandments broken,
  Emblems of the taint within.

Thorns and weeds in EDEN grew not,
  There no fitting soil they found;
Toil like this our parents knew not,
  Dwelling on that holy ground.

Until they, from GOD estrangèd,
  Into disobedience ran;—
Then all Nature's face was changèd,
  Changèd most the heart of man.

For his sin the earth was blighted—
  Thorns and thistles it must bear;
On man's heart the curse alighted,
  Bringing sorrow, toil, and care!

" Roots of bitterness" are springing
  Where the plants of love had place;
Earthly passions, closely clinging,
  Check the growth of heavenly Grace;

Sweet Affections, wildly playing,
  Take some holier Duty's room;
Virtues, from their stations straying,
  Waste, like idle weeds, their bloom.

Ah! what anxious watchful training
  Does the heart of Christian need;
Wild luxuriance restraining,
  Rooting out the intruding weed.

Care of parent and of pastor
  Thorn and thistle must remove ;
While the garden's heavenly Master
  Prunes each plant with hand of love.

Thus I mused within my garden,
  Bearing of man's fall the trace ;
Conscious of the need of pardon,
  Longing for refreshing grace.

Oh ! might I, each power improving,
  Training still to duty's scope,
From my heart all ill removing,
  Work in Faith, and rest in Hope ;—

Hope to see *that* garden flourish,
  Lovely with immortal bloom,
Where no weed the soil shall nourish,
  Thorn nor brier shall have room.

There no sin, no care invadeth,
  There no sorrow ever trod ;
Where the blossom never fadeth,
  In the Paradise of God !

"NO MORE!"

OR, FAITH.

NO MORE! Oh, saddest words that can be
    spoken,
    How heavy fall ye on the painèd ear!
Telling of cherish'd hopes for ever broken,
    Sounding the knell of joys we've held most dear!

Sad, when the friends of youth have been estrangèd,
    The hearts which once were warm to us grown
      cold,
The eyes, the voices, once familiar, changèd,
    No more to greet us as they did of old.

Sad, when the hands, long link'd in ours, still pressing,
    Of friends departing for some distant shore,
With throbbing heart we hear, we breathe the bles-
    sing,
    " Farewell! God speed you! We may meet no
      more!"

Oh, sadder yet, as fast the life is fleeting,
    And now well-nigh some loved one's course is o'er,

L

Watching how faint, how slow the pulse is beating,
  To feel, to know at length, it beats *no more!*

Saddest, when o'er the dead the earth is closing,
  To think, as on the dust the dust is thrown,
We can recall *no more* the friend we're losing,
  We can behold *no more* the form that's gone!

Such, while we linger in this earthy dwelling,
  O'erburthen'd with our tenement of clay,
The thoughts which in our bosoms will be swelling,
  Of hopeless loss—of unrepair'd decay.

But such may not be always;—nor may sadness
  Thus *ever* dwell in the desponding breast;—
Far brighter hopes should cheer our hearts to gladness,
  Hopes of eternal joys, of endless rest.

No MORE! Oh, sweetest sounds which shall be
      spoken,
  How on the charmèd ear shall ye descend,
Telling of sorrow's chain for ever broken,
  Breathing of pleasures which shall never end!

Oh, words of glorious promise! for the portals
  Of Death, which close so darkly on us here,
Shall ope, *no more to close,* on us immortals,
  Heirs of the blessings of a heavenly sphere.

There, friend *no more* shall be from friend estrangèd,
    Love, pure and holy, shall unite them still;
No more affection shall be chill'd or changèd,
    Where nor deceit can be, nor thought of ill.

There, friend *no more* from friend shall distance sever,
    No sad farewells shall rend the throbbing heart;
Join'd in the service of their GOD for ever,
    Nor death nor absence shall those spirits part.

There, no more shall be sorrow, no more crying,—
    For GOD shall wipe all tears from every eye;
There, no more shall be felt the fear of dying,
    For CHRIST hath died, that we *no more* should die!

" No MORE!" oh, blessed words, which shall be
      spoken,
    Telling that sin and sorrow's reign is o'er,—
That Hell's dominion is *for ever* broken,—
    That we can sin, can weep, can die *no more!*

HOPE on! Hope ever! While the sun
    shines brightly,
    While youth and joy have sway within
    thy breast :—
While the fresh turf thy footstep presseth lightly,
   And care hath not disturb'd thy bosom's rest :—
        Hope on!
What though the shadows of impending sorrow
   Too soon shall rise, and darken round thy way :—
Hope on! Hope ever on! that each to-morrow
   May be as bright and joyous as to-day.
        Hope ever on!

Hope on! Hope ever! When those shades shall
    darken,
   And man's inheritance of woe be thine;
Still to the cheering voice of comfort hearken,
   And mark beneath the clouds the sunbeams shine!
        Hope on!
What though that cheering voice may be mistaken—
   What though the sunbeam fades in night away ;—

Hope on! Hope ever on! with faith unshaken,
 To-morrow may be brighter than to-day!
   Hope ever on!

Hope on! Hope ever! though the road be dreary,—
 Though lights that cheer'd and guided thee be
   gone,—
Though thy heart sicken, and thy feet be weary,—
 Cheer up, faint heart! and weary feet, toil on!
   Hope on!
What though the gloom more close appears to gather,
 And every step appears beset with harm :—
Hope on! Hope ever on! thy loving Father
 Will clear thy sight, and shield thee with His
   arm!
    Hope ever on!

Hope on! Hope ever! when this vale of sorrow
 Shall lead thee to the vale of deeper shade ;
How bright the prospect gleams on *that* to-morrow
 Of deathless life, of joys that cannot fade!
   Hope on!
What though the gloom hangs deeper o'er the portal,
 Yet feet divine the darksome path have trod ;—
Hope on! Hope ever on! with love immortal,
 And Faith all centred on the Son of God!
   Hope ever on!

ONWARD! YET NOT ALONE;

OR, CHARITY.

" How beautiful and grand is the idea of the no longer
" solitary ascent of the mountains of difficulty; each climber
" helping up also a little company, bearing the ' Banner with
" the strange device.' "—Mrs. Grant.

ONWARD! yet not alone,
   For other feet must tread the narrow way,
     To whom, as cheerfully thou toilest on,
Thy hand may be a comfort and a stay.

   Forward! though rough the road,
And though thy burden heavy on thee lie;
   Yet each may help his brother with his load,
And feel his own the lighter made thereby!

   Upward! the path is wild!
But not for toil thy efforts may be stay'd;
   The gentle maiden and the tender child
Lean on thine hand, and look to thee for aid.

Onward! though dark the day,
And though the storm appears to gather round;—
Behind the clouds behold a brighter ray,
And cheer the weak ones with a hopeful sound!

Forward! be firm and bold!
For weary, resting on the wayside stone,
The tender woman and the grandsire old
Have toil'd before thee; thou must help them on!

Upward! the thankful smile
Of those who know the dangers thou hast past,
And converse sweet, shall the steep way beguile,
Until thou reach the home of Rest at last.

Onward! the way is long!
The weakly ones will feel their strength decay;—
That thou may'st comfort them, thy heart is strong,
Thy hand is nerved, to give them needful stay!

Forward! thou may'st not rest!
The toil thou bearest is a toil of love:—
Who helpeth others shall himself be blest
With peace, and light, and strengthening from above.

Then upward! not alone!
For weaker feet the rugged path have trod,
Have cheer'd each other as they journey'd on,
Depending on their Saviour and their GOD!

NOTES.

NOTES.

¹ PAGE 21.

THIS poem, and the one that follows it, were composed when the author was in a more classical atmosphere than he has since enjoyed; but he has no reference now to the book where he met with the tradition. This stanza, however, was added lately, and the idea was borrowed from the description in the Iliad, B. ix. lines 185-191. The following lines are from a translation by T. S. Brandreth, printed in 1845, which is more close to the original than Pope's verfion :—

" But when they reach'd the Myrmidons' fair tents,
" They found him his soul soothing with the lyre,
" Which, fair and varied, with a filver yoke,
" He took when he Eetion's city spoil'd.
" On this he sang the glorious deeds of men;
" Alone Patroclus near in silence sat,
" Waiting, till Peleus' son should cease from song."

Eetion, the father of Andromache, was king of Thebæ in Cilicia, and was killed by Achilles.

[2] PAGE 23.

This Ballad is founded on a passage in the Persæ of Æschylus, l. 401, &c., where the Battle of Salamis is described.

[3] PAGE 25.

The Legend of O'Donohue, on which this poem is founded, is contained in T. Crofton Croker's " Fairy Legends of Ireland."

[4] PAGE 32.

These stanzas were composed about the years 1832-3, when the Author resided in the immediate neighbourhood of the Giants' Causeway. It was at first intended to continue the subject, so as to embrace more of the remarkable scenery belonging to the rocky coast, of which some striking features and legends connected with them are here noticed ; but removal from the place interrupted the intention, and other occupations prevented its being resumed. The poem, as it is, however, includes most of the points of interest seen by ordinary visitors.

[5] PAGE 32.

Lucretius, B. ii. 1-10.

[6] PAGE 35.

Fionn M'Coul, or M'Comhal, commonly called Fingal, is the great hero of Irish mythology, according to which he is claimed as an *Irish* monarch, who invaded and conquered the western coasts of Scotland.

This tradition differs from Macpherson's Ossian, according to which he was a Scottish prince; but many places, named in the supposed poems of Ossian, can be identified in the north of Ireland. " Innisfail" is a name of Ireland; " Morven," the west of Scotland. The tradition of the " Causeway" having been made from Ireland to Staffa, by Fingal, and afterwards destroyed by him, is one of the wild stories of the coast.

[7] PAGE 36.

Luno, according to Macpherson's Ossian, was Fingal's smith; whence his sword is called " the blade of dark brown Luno."

[8] PAGE 36.

" The Loom " is the name given to a colonnade of basaltic pillars at the south-eastern side of the Giants' Causeway; the pillars are about forty feet high. It is impossible to assign any reason for the name, except some fancied likeneſs, which has been here fancifully adopted.

[8] PAGE 36.

The basalt, of which the columns and many other rocks at the Giants' Causeway consist, is of a flinty hardness, and is incapable of being wrought by stonecutters into shape, as it flies in all directions from the tool.

[10] PAGE 37.

" There are two very distinct and opposite theories of the formation of basalt, called the Plutonian and Neptunian, the one attributing its origin to fire, the

other to water."—*Guide to the Giants' Causeway, by the*
REV. G. N. WRIGHT, 1823, pages 101 to 109, where
the two theories and that of crystallization are discussed.

" PAGE 37.

" The Giant's Chair " is a large rock, bearing a
rude resemblance to a chair, near high-water mark,
and a short distance from the east side of the Causeway, commanding a good prospect of this natural mole,
as it stretches its length of 300 yards with a gentle
slope into the sea.   I take the opportunity here of
naming briefly some of the places alluded to in the following stanzas.   On the east of the causeway is a wide
bay, called Port Noffer, properly Port na Fhair, the
Man's or *Giant's* Bay.   Near its centre " *the Shepherd's
path* " winds up the slopes, and conducts to the top of
the cliffs.   Eastward, this bay is terminated by the steep
headland called by guides Rovinvally, properly, Rue-
hen-valla, the *cliff at the head of the wall;* dividing it
from the " Giants' *Theatre,*" or Port Reostan (meaning
not known), a deep and narrow bay, with almost pre-
cipitous sides, and two fine ranges of columns.   The
eastern boundary of this bay is called the " Chimney-
headland," from two or three insulated pillars; below
this, Port Madh-a-ruagh, the bay of *the red fox ;* and,
close adjoining, Port na Spania, or *Spanish* bay, separated by the headland Ben-an-ouran (meaning not
known) from another small bay or two ; in one of which
are some pillars of extraordinary size, *not jointed,* as
others along these cliffs are.   The other boundary of
these bays is Plaiskin, or the *dry-headland ;* the highest

and most remarkable cliff of the range : but the finest
view of it is from Benbawn, the *white-head*, a little
more to the east, which commands some of the most
striking features of the whole coast.

[12] PAGE 37.

There is, or was, a footpath, used occasionally by
shepherds in search of stray sheep, or by guides in
search of spars, steatite, and other *specimens*, going
round all the faces of the cliffs and recesses of the bays ;
a course full of interest, and not without the excitement
of danger.

[13] PAGE 39.

When I first visited these headlands, in 1824, there
was a tradition well authenticated, that, three or four
years before, a young gentleman, a tourist, having by
some accident got upon the track mentioned in the
last note, came by it to the insulated columns called
the " chimneys," and having climbed to the base of
them, about 300 feet above the sea, left on the lowest,
just within his reach, his *glove*, and a piece of money,
to be earned by whoever would fetch it.

[14] PAGE 39.

Port na Spania is so called from the tradition that
one of the ships of the Armada, driven hither by the
storm which dispersed that fleet, was wrecked in this
bay, on a rock, covered at high water, still called the
Spanish rock. The shattered appearance of the Chimney
rocks is fancifully attributed to the Spaniards having

fired at and overthrown some of the range, mistaking them for towers of Dunluce Castle.

[15] PAGE 41.

Dunseverick Castle, now but a small ruin, but once a place of strength, stands on a steep rock, in a narrow bay, about three miles to the east of these headlands.

[16] PAGE 42.

The story of Adam Morning is to be found in Dr. Hamilton's " Letters from the Coast of Antrim." It happened above seventy years ago, but was well remembered, as here described, when I first knew the scene of the occurrence. In Port na Spania is a re-markable range of pillars, enclosed on each side by the sloping of the banks, so as to look like the pipes of an *organ*. There is another, better known, in Port Noffer. From the summit of the cliff a perilous path descends; and on the very top of *the Organ* a long step must be made, where a false step would probably be fatal. Here Morning fell, and died: and here, in 1834, a poor woman, whom I knew, fell over with a burden of sea-weed, and was taken up for dead, but having only a rib or two broken, she recovered; and, strange to say, frequently climbed the same path afterwards.

[17] PAGE 43.

The Rev. Dr. William Hamilton, a clergyman of the diocese of Armagh, who was barbarously mur-dered at his own house in 1798, was one of the first persons who drew public attention to the wonders of

the Giants' Causeway, by his " Letters from Antrim." He had a hut erected during one summer on
Benbawn, from which it is still called " Hamilton's
seat;" and the fruit of his sojourn there was a model
in wood of the headland Plaiskin, still in the Museum
of Trinity College, Dublin.

[18] PAGE 43.

It is common with guides, and it enhances the sur-
prising effect of the view, to bring visitors by a path at
a little distance from the cliffs to this point, and to keep
them (if possible) from looking round, till they come
to the spot where the whole is at once displayed before
them.

[19] PAGE 45.

This poem, composed in early youth, is little more
than the version of a legend which appeared about
the year 1825 in the Literary Gazette. The same
story has also been printed in an Irish Magazine, about
twenty years ago; and has lately formed the subject
of a poem called " the Bell-founder," by Mr. C.
M'Carthy.

[20] PAGE 50.

Glen-da-lough, the *Glen* of *two Lakes*, was chosen
by St. Kevin, a man of noble family, as the site of a
religious establishment, towards the end of the sixth
century. He first dwelt in the upper part of the valley; partly in the cave called Kevin's Bed, and partly
at a church, now quite ruined, called Temple na
Skellig, or the church in the wilderness. From this he

removed to a church, near the junction of the Two Lakes, and where the stream from the waterfall of Poolanass flows towards the lower, which is now called " the Rhefeart," or *kings' burying-place*, because several of the kings of that country were buried there. The building, as usual with *very old* Irish churches, was very small, and is now ruinous; but its doorway presents the characteristics of very great antiquity, as does also that of " Our Lady's Church," which attracted the peculiar admiration of Sir Walter Scott. The stone-roofed building, called " Kevin's kitchen," is to be referred to the same period, and " it may reasonably be believed," says Mr. Petrie, " that it was the *residence* of the founder of Glen-da-lough, when he removed from his seclusion near the Upper Lake." The " Cathedral," if not built before the death of Kevin, in 618, cannot have been much later; and the round Tower, and Trinity Church, are of a similar date. In the course of the seventh century Glen-da-lough became a city, of which only the *arched gateway* remains; and a seminary was founded, from which were sent forth many exemplary men, who diffused the light of religion around the western world. From the year 770 to 1020, it was repeatedly taken and plundered by the Danes; it suffered severely in the various troubles of Ireland; and it was finally burnt and destroyed in 1398, and never recovered its overthrow.

[21] PAGE 53.

The story from which this Ballad (written in 1828) is taken may be found in Sharon Turner's " History of the Anglo-Saxons," B. III. Ch. vii. It has also furnished the subject for a poem in the " Lays and Ballads of Early English History," by my brother, the Rev. Frederick W. Mant; each of us having written in entire ignorance of the other's having taken the same subject.

[22] PAGE 67.

A beautiful poem on the same story was published, in 1830, by Mrs. Hemans, in " Records of Woman, and other poems." Had I seen it, these stanzas might perhaps not have been written; but, though only in MS. till now, they were composed in 1829.

[23] PAGE 73.

This poem was suggested by the description of the discovery by Copernicus of the true theory of the solar system, in Professor O. M. Mitchell's " Planetary and Stellar Worlds." The *facts* are stated as briefly as possible, in the introduction to the poem; but it is only fair to acknowledge my obligations to Mr. Mitchell, by quoting at more length a few sentences, of which I have tried to embody the ideas. " Long did the philosopher hesitate, perplexed with doubts, surrounded by prejudice, embarrassed with difficulties; but finally rising superior to every consideration save truth, he quitted the earth, swept boldly through space, and *planted himself upon the sun.* With an imagination endowed with most extraordinary tenacity, he carried with him all the phenomena of the heavens, so familiar to his eye when viewed from the earth. . . . He commences with his now distant earth: its immobility is gone. . . . He gives his attention to the planets; their complex wanderings, their stations, their retrograde motions, all disappeared, and he beheld them sweeping harmoniously around him . . . all moving in the same direction, their paths filling the same belt of the heavens. . . . This beautiful system, far from perfect, was founded in truth; and although improvement might and must come, revolution could never shake its firm foundation."

The expressions in the last stanza are similar to those recorded of *Kepler*; but they are quite as agreeable to the patient and pious character of his great predecessor.

[24] PAGE 85.

In reading Herrick's " Litany to the Holy Spirit" I had often felt that it was rather suited to a death-bed, or a sick-bed at least, than to the ordinary wants of a Christian's life. Such a sentiment led to the composition of the present " Litany;" and the belief that the wants and aspirations it expresses are common to man may be enough to justify its publication.

[25] PAGE 106.

The allusion is to Bion's " Epitaph on Moschus."

[26] PAGE 106.

See Beattie's " Minstrel," Book I. Stanza xxvii.

" Shall I be left forgotten in the dust,
    " When Fate, relenting, lets the flower revive ?
" ShallNature's voice, to man alone unjust,

" Bid him, though doom'd to perish, hope to live ?
" Is it for this fair Virtue oft must strive
" With disappointment, penury, and pain ?
" No : Heaven's immortal spring shall yet arrive,
" And man's majestic beauty bloom again,
" Bright through th' eternal year of Love's triumphant
     reign."

[27] PAGE 116.

This poem, and the one before it, were composed on
the separation of a party of six, after three weeks spent
happily in each other's company. While these pages
were preparing for the press, I met with a passage in
Sir E. B. Lytton's " What will he do with It ? "
part of which I venture to quote as embodying the same
or similar thoughts. " There is one warning lesson in
life, which few of us have not received, and no book
that I can call to memory has noted down with an
adequate emphasis. It is this, ' Beware of parting !'
The true sadness is not in the pain of parting; it is in
the When and the How you are to meet again with the
face about to vanish from your view. . . . Meet again
you may ; will it be in the same way ? with the same
sympathies ? with the same sentiments ? Will the souls
hurrying on in diverse paths unite once more, as if the
interval had been a dream ? Rarely, rarely !. . . . Are
you happy in the spot on which you tarry with the
persons whose voices are now melodious to your ears ?
Beware of parting ; or, if part you must, say not, in
insolent defiance to Time and Destiny, ' What matters ?
we shall soon meet again !'"

———

[28] PAGE 121.

These lines were composed above thirty years ago,
after a conversation with a friend, in which we had
quoted and commented on the poem of Byron beginning,

" There's not a joy the world can give, like that it
        takes away, &c."

and several expressions will be found to allude to lines
in that poem.

[29] PAGE 128.

Sca-Fell Pikes is the name of the highest mountain
in the lake country of Cumberland and Westmoreland.
It has two summits, of which the highest is called *Pikes*,
and the other, but little lower, is *Sca-Fell*. They are
separated by a wide, deep, and dark chasm, called
Mickle Door; and I remember being forcibly reminded
of the

" Heights that appear as lovers who have parted
" In hate, whose mining depths so intervene,
    " That they can meet no more, though broken-
        hearted,"

in " Childe Harold," Canto III. St. xciv.

The " Star grass," in page 129, is the local name of
the *Parnassia Palustris*, or Grass of Parnassus.

[30] PAGE 130.

I am bound in justice to acknowledge that some of
the thoughts, and even some expressions in this little

poem, were derived from a beautiful child's book, called, "The Story without an End," translated from the German by Mrs. Austin.

[31] PAGE 133.

The scene is Sandymount Strand, in Dublin Bay, where I was staying when this poem was composed. The Bailey Lighthouse, under the hill of Howth, has a steady light towards the sea ; and the harbour light, at Kingstown, on the south side of the Bay, shows alternately red and white. In the centre of the bay, near the channel of the Liffey, is a third lighthouse, connected by a long wall or causeway with the Pigeon House Fort, and showing a steady bright light all round.

FINIS.

CHISWICK PRESS :—PRINTED BY WHITTINGHAM AND WILKINS, TOOKS COURT, CHANCERY LANE.